THE WIDENING

THE WIDENING

a novel by
CAROL MOLDAW

etruscan press

Etruscan Press
Wilkes University
84 West South Street
Wilkes-Barre, PA 18766

Moldaw, Carol.
    The Widening / Carol Moldaw.
    p. cm.
    ISBN-13: 978-0-9745995-9-5
    ISBN-10: 0-9745995-9-X

    1. Young women--Sexual behavior--Fiction. 2. Young
women--Psychology--Fiction. 3. Sex--United States--
Fiction. 4. Bildungsromans.   I. Title.

    PS3563.O392W53 2008   813'.54
                        QBI07-600326
Interior design by Sarah Quaranta
Cover design by Nicole DePolo
Cover art *Desirous 8* by Rikki Ducornet

The publication of *The Widening* has been made possible by a grant from
the National Endowment for the Arts.

NATIONAL
ENDOWMENT
FOR THE ARTS

A great nation
deserves great art.

ACKNOWLEDGMENTS

Grateful acknowledgment is made to the editors of the following publications in which portions of The Widening originally appeared: *AGNI, American Letters & Commentary, Chokecherries, Conjunctions, StoryQuarterly,* and the anthology *Never Before: Poems about First Experiences* (Four Way Books, 2005).

I would also like to thank Martha Collins, Lavinia Currier, Sandy Dijkstra, Rikki Ducornet, Myra Goldberg, Jeffrey Gustavson, Jill Marsal, Jim Moore, Andrew McCord, Jackie Osherow, Miriam Sagan, Jennifer Stroup, Arthur Sze, Barbara Tedlock, and Caroline Thompson, all of whom gave me essential encouragement and discernment in the writing of this book.

Part One

"I had rather have a fool to make me merry than experience to make me sad--and to travel for it too!"

—As You Like It

One

At the crucial moment she said yes. His hand in the back pocket of her jeans had made her wet—but nothing and no one had prepared her. They were on her bed, at boarding school. Naked she was self-conscious, and self-conscious she was timid. He would know what to do if only she let him. She remembered letting herself be kissed when she was twelve, pulled into the bushes by a classmate, happily ambushed, titillated, but sure right up until the moment his lips pressed hers that she would not be kissed, no matter how long they sat nested in the shrubs, because it was forbidden. He dug in, the sharp pain snapping her out of her reverie, and knowing she could not bear it if she conceived, she said no, pushing his shoulders hard with her hands. At once he was out, up, and through the door. Why had he left? In the bathroom, she looked and saw what she'd heard she'd find: blood. Her body pounded and throbbed, with the widening had come a great unremitting pressure on her bones and she ached inside. And that was it, she'd lost something she'd not examined having, something that until then had seemed irrelevant, illusory.

Two

One Wednesday she took the bus to a nearby town and went to Planned Parenthood. The clinic was not on the main street, nor in the mall, but out by used-car lots, mechanics, and a veterinarian. She could hear the whiz of traffic on the freeway to her right, and she played a balancing game on the raised curb. There was no sidewalk, only the four-lane road and gravel. She was following directions a girl in the dorm had given her. After the physical exam, the doctor stood, took off his gloves, and asked her questions. She moved her feet out of the stirrups, crossed her dangling ankles, and squirmed to adjust her paper gown. He wanted to know how long she had known her boyfriend, what kind of relationship she was in, what kind of birth control she preferred, what her previous experience was, what were her feelings? She drew into herself the way a hermit crab retracts into its borrowed shell and displays nothing of its own, but she couldn't help crying. The box of Kleenex was on a counter out of reach. The doctor said he was refusing her the diaphragm she wanted because she had no boyfriend, but he would give her a six-month renewable supply of 80 mg Norinyl. He lectured her on sexual mores and handed her the sheets of Kleenex one by one, as she reached for them.

Three

He couldn't believe his bad luck, that she was so close to being a virgin, but wasn't one. He liked to tease her about it, to gripe that she was second-hand goods. When she first noticed him, he was staring at her in the cafeteria all through dinner. Later, she saw him playing with the faculty dogs. One afternoon she went to his room and devised a collage of his face for an art class assignment. She had meant only to flirt, and to keep her advantage of indifference. In a magazine she'd found four small torpedoes to use as his eyebrows. He heated water on his hot plate and fixed them hot chocolate with rum. She wasn't good at drawing, but in the end it looked like him, and felt like him, a mixture of a bulldog's bravado and a sheepdog's sleepy warmth. He was more courtly, nicer than she'd expected. Before she left, he opened the curtains and they saw it was snowing. She hadn't been in snow since she was six; it dazzled her, obliterating the last of her resistance. Over the holiday break, at home, she wrote in her journal obsessively, but didn't consult anyone. Even the mysterious red spots that broke out up and down her body couldn't dissuade her.

Four

The thing she remembered best about their first time together was that the next morning her father picked her up on his way to the state democratic convention in Sacramento. She was wearing a brightly embroidered Mexican blouse. A colleague of his was also in the car, but he couldn't contain his fury when he saw she had thrown her clothes for the weekend into an open woven basket. They waited in the car while she went back into the dorm to repack her clothes, putting them into a zippered bag. Finally they left. For most of the three-hour trip she dozed in the backseat. In the convention hall, she sat with her head in her arms at one of the long tables and daydreamed. This too made her father furious. They were sharing a room, and she felt uncomfortable in his presence, as if he would know, or worse, ask, the way a year earlier he had asked, during dinner with another family, if she had ever smoked marijuana. They had been on vacation in Mexico. She had not lied, and when her father blew up at her, she had fled to the bathroom and cried until the son from the other family came to console and brace her. The next day, her mother sequestered herself in bed. She doubted she would tell the truth now. On the drive back, just the two of them, she let the wind pick up her hair and caress her face as she listened to him silently. He enjoyed talking and, as if responding to the confidence she hadn't made, was telling her about his own early sexual experience, about Jill Moss, the unfortunate girl all the boys knew about, and his conviction that promiscuous people were unhappy. The only thing, he wondered, was whether they were promiscuous because they were unhappy, or unhappy because they were promiscuous? Never considering, she thought to herself, that perhaps they weren't unhappy at all.

Five

He told her to move her hips, but she was afraid she would go wild and he would malign her. When she told him she wasn't sure what he meant, how to move them, he believed her and let it go. She was content: passivity had made her patient, dreamy. Sometimes they would escape to his room during the school's morning assembly, before her math class, even though afterwards it was hard to adjust to her teacher's rat-a-tat style, hard not to feel exposed, her underpants soaked. Once she saw that not too much would be demanded of her, she was able to relax. The course of their lovemaking was dictated by the mercurial rise and fall of his penis, but lying underneath him, couching him, she felt mild rustlings that sometimes grew in urgency. Usually she stifled these before they overwhelmed her. Only once, as they lay together resting, did she continue rocking, rubbing against his thigh. Moving away, he snickered, and made much of her trying to hump him shamelessly, like a dog.

Six

If you have to ask, you haven't had one. Using the doorknob as a barre, the girl in the plum-colored leotard squatted slightly to make a plié, then straightened and curved one leg up, first in front, for an attitude *devant*, and then behind, for an attitude *derrière*, having been at boarding school long enough to know at least what to pretend to know, and how to bring it off. The other girls nodded. They were lounging in the open center of the dorm. *It's like riding a wave,* said one, a veil of smoke rising from where she lay on the floor. A long-lashed girl sitting on the arm of the couch reached down, took a drag, and demurred as she exhaled, *It's like being the wave.* Now that the fire had sparked, the others piled on their tributes: *It's like a volcano erupting . . . like riding a horse and breaking into a canter . . . like whirling colors in a kaleidoscope . . . like time stopping . . . like nothing else at all.* Then they ended where they had begun, vigorously agreeing, *You'll know.* But what she thought she might know already, the girls' metaphysics only made her question more.

Seven

He told her she had a hot box. A pungent smell. He told her that from now on her body would need it, that she'd be like an addict. That she'd do it herself when no one else was there to. It was spring and the hills, like those she knew so well across the bay, would soon turn brown. Two weeks and he would be going east: home for the summer, and to college in the fall. He told her to come visit him. His mother would call and placate her parents. She could stay in his sister's old room. He would show her New York. She felt trapped in his grip, in the closed air of his room, trapped by his plans, words, breath, as if his breath, not her own, was what kept her alive, weakened and poisoned. She twisted away from him to face the window; she stared at the hills as he kept talking. Two weeks. Two weeks and she'd be free.

Eight

Experimenting, first she slipped her finger in and out. Then she kept it still inside her, rotating around it, like water lapping around an oar. Lifting her hand, she looked at the filmy liquid. She smelled and tasted it before tucking her hand back between her legs. Rocking on her stomach, she slipped her finger in and out again, rhythmically, in a trance. When she heard her sister go into the bathroom, on the other side of the wall her headboard leaned against, she automatically froze, and listened to the sounds of water: water in the tap, water being swished into the sink, water fountaining into water, water being flushed. Gingerly, quietly, she touched the bump outside her vagina. It was hard like a pebble, but soft and slippery. Finally, her sister was gone. Waves upon waves broke open inside her. The breath of roses sweetened the room. On the other side of a garden, through an open gate, her body had its own volition. She was relieved that it could override her mind, because it was her mind she didn't trust, her mind, self-conscious and fearful, that trapped her. It was comforting to know this power her body had, and to give herself over in the safety, the aloneness, of her own bed. When she drew her finger out it was pale and wrinkled, as if she had been in the bath too long. She dried it on the bedsheet and fell asleep.

Nine

In the afternoon, done for the day with her summer job shelving books at the library, she waited on a park bench for him to pick her up, or walked down the block, where she'd discreetly parked her mother's baby-blue Mercedes, and drove to where he was house-sitting. He was a friend of her sister's boyfriend. The great torpor she had felt at school, like the weight of water, submerging, even swallowing her, had subsided, and now, being with him, she was light and happy. He would nuzzle her face with closed lips. He would brush her hair and smooth his hand against her nape, and then kiss it. She had been glad to share with him what she'd found on her own, and he reciprocated, praising her, showing her a self she'd never seen. She liked the way, praising her face, her breasts, her belly, her lips, her ankles, her thighs, his hands anticipated, kindled the words. He also praised her laugh, her voice, the way she thought about things, expressed herself, understood him, touched him, and could soothe him. The day before the family came back to reclaim their home, while they were stripping the bed, and then later, when they remade it with clean sheets, returning to its place the bedspread they had kept folded on an armchair, she felt the way she used to feel packing her trunk at the end of camp each summer: uneasy, disconsolate. She cheered herself up a little by leafing through the book of pop philosophy he'd given her for her seventeenth birthday, *Be Here Now*. He himself had just turned twenty. Again and again, she flipped to the front to study his inscription: *I love you. Never change.*

Ten

Months afterward she found out that his mother had had a nervous breakdown, and his brother had tried to kill himself, or maybe it was the other way around, but at the end of the summer, when he stopped calling, she could think of no reason. She couldn't think at all. She sat by the phone; she made spells; she tried the force of her will upon the open lines of the empty air. She listened to the silence intently, observantly, but still could not find its reason, could not find its edge. She had trusted her feelings; what was she to trust now? Finally, she capitulated. He answered coldly, and was incommunicative, as if there was no bond between them. And what did he owe her? Although she was conscientious toward others, toward herself she didn't want anyone to feel an obligation. The very idea that he might think she was trying to press a claim upon him mortified her. She wanted his actions to be motivated by love; she wanted to be his ally even in his desertion of her, for in her mind it brought them closer. He would think well of her if she understood what he couldn't explain. She squeezed her feelings down until they fit inside her beliefs, the way you can cram a drawer full and then slowly push it shut, though later you may have to pull and pry and use all your strength to get it open.

Eleven

They talked and talked and talked, sitting for hours in her girlfriend's red velvet easy chairs, smoking Camel straights, drinking coffee, sometimes whiskey, their cups, ashtrays, books, all balanced on the wide, flat armrests. She admired everything about this girl to whom she could listen endlessly, just as, when younger, she had read books for hours on end. It seemed to her that her friend—even with her jellied diaphragm slipping through her fingers like a fish, even on acid at eleven years old (was or wasn't it rape?), despite sleeping with their newly married drama teacher—it seemed she never lost her self-possession. Practicing Spanish together, they read Neruda out loud, then showed each other their own poems, which wafted across the page trailing pale chiffon scarves and rose petals. She decided it must have been the poems that led this knowing girl to pick her out, because next to her she felt inarticulate, awkward, untried. She was not theatrical, and could not build up her experience in words convincingly enough to sustain a leading role at the center of her own imagination. She became her friend's understudy, mouthing words, practicing bold gestures in her chair.

Twelve

She rode into the city with two classmates. Although her own attempt to find an internship at a letterpress had fallen through, she wanted to see the Victorian house where seniors could spend a semester while they worked at hospitals or soup kitchens or avant-garde theater companies. The boy who drove was tall and rangy, with a good-natured guffaw; the girl, a friend she sometimes went bicycling with in lieu of PE. As the house had no extra beds for visitors, they were given three blankets, shown the downstairs bathroom, and left to themselves in the living room as others went upstairs to sleep. When they settled in for the night, bunched together on the rug, he was in the middle. She could barely let herself breathe, her breath sounded so loud to her, each slightly rasping outtake of air like a breeze billowing open the flimsy curtain she had pulled across her heart. Did her breath smell? Did she? Mortified by the thought, she let out a long sigh, which somehow drew him in, and their legs brushed. The girl on his other side seemed to be asleep. She had imagined being even nearer to him than this, she had imagined him sneaking into her dorm past the teacher on night duty, stopping at her room, turning the knob without knocking, kissing her until she woke, though she would have been awake already, slipping into bed beside her, wordless, the way others did in the stories she heard every morning. She had imagined someday they would meet in the lobby of an old hotel in a foreign country, a country at war. She would know him right away, but he wouldn't have recognized her, if it hadn't been for her by-line. She had become so beautiful, so striking. Or had she always been, he would try to remember, wondering how he could have forgotten. Because he had always been lovelorn for another, had never seen—had—he was grasping her now, kissing her, touching, and still she worried about her breath, about how she seemed, compared to others, especially that one other, and did he notice her fat, did her breasts seem funny to him, laughable, did he like her touch, did it make any difference, did he care? Now her breath *was* sounding loud, now the curtain surely was torn, now she had to hush herself—and now that it was over, what would it change?

Thirteen

She sat on the hill and watched the moon emerge as the sky deepened. She sat alone on the hill and looked down at the dormitory, at the yellow square of light behind his curtains. She sat alone on the bare field of the hill and stared into this yellow square of light until she was so frazzled her concentration broke. She walked down the gentle slope of the hill past his dormitory to her own, into her room, turned on the yellow light, and drew the curtains. She sat at her desk and opened her notebook. She wrote nothing. She closed the book and stared at the wall. She lay on her side on the single bed, her notebook open beside her. She scrawled her name. His name. Her name. His. She heard voices in the hall. It was time for dinner. She walked out of her room as naturally as she could, shutting the door behind her, letting herself be caught up in the protective swarm of chattering girls.

Fourteen

In the spring semester, she decided, she would go to Spain. In Spain, she wouldn't know anyone. No one person's not calling, no one person's touch, no one person's breath or heartbeat binding her, slave, shadow, child. She thought it out one evening at her desk, daydreaming instead of studying. She had enough credits to graduate, but would enroll in a school to avoid living with a family. One family was enough. Writing to tell her oldest friend, she felt inspired, and invited her to come to Spain too. They could start off at the school, and then they could travel together. They wouldn't need an itinerary. They wouldn't travel like conventional tourists, like her parents, making plans and reservations, sticking to fixed ideas about where to go, where to stay, which museums, parks, and churches not to miss, where to eat, the hour, what to order, and the next day, what to admire, what to buy. She thought that if you culled and clipped your ideas from *Gourmet* magazine and the Sunday *Times* travel section, then you left no room for the experience itself—for its adventure. They would learn as they went along. They would come and go as it pleased them, without interference, without authorization or guidance. She knew this would appeal to her friend. Writing about it gave her confidence, and transformed what had seemed a wild daydream into a definite plan, with its own independent logic and momentum.

Fifteen

Just before she left, he came back, professing his love. He came back, like an abject puppy, to nuzzle her cheek, to burrow into her. He didn't want her to go. Her head on his shoulder, his hand in her hair, she listened absently while he told a vague, confusing story about his mother and brother. She had to admit to herself she was deliriously glad to see him, to have him drive all the way from Santa Cruz—from college—to visit her for the weekend. She was happy; she liked sheltering him from school officials while flaunting his presence in front of students. She liked the intimacy of sharing her room with him, of falling asleep and waking up tangled together in the narrow single bed. It was nice to feel beloved again, to stroke and be stroked. When they made love she felt a sea of ice begin to break up inside her. Salt caught in their throats; salt tears from every pore, from her opening, cleansed and renewed them. So she was surprised to remember, lying next to him, becalmed, that she was about to flout this happiness, to shun it, to let it drop to the floor carelessly, like an old blouse, or a pair of Levi's that would only get better the worse she treated them.

Sixteen

In Spain, she wore her knowing attitude proudly, like a class ring, but when she turned it back and forth on her finger, calling attention to it, exaggerating its importance to her, that was when she felt most nervous and at sea. Some mornings, she walked from the school's apartment building on the seaside of town, through the dusty square to the open market at its far edge, and bought bread and figs or corn nuts. Once she caught a Spanish boy mimicking the loose way she swung her arms, and from then on she couldn't move naturally, couldn't remember how to coordinate her arms and legs. Did the left arm go forward with the right leg, or could it just stay put? She tested different gaits, and scrutinized herself walking by the café with the plate-glass windows. She could see that she had gained weight, even her baggy black Big Ben work pants couldn't hide that. She had gained weight, though she was smoking a lot, smoking the strong Spanish tobacco called black tobacco, stronger even than Gauloises. Still, she was sure it wasn't the cigarettes, but the effort to speak Spanish at the café, post office, market, bar, even at school, that was constricting her throat so that she could barely speak at all. And the quieter she became, the rounder she grew, the slower she walked, the more reflexively she smoked, the more knowing and calm people found her, the more her deep brown eyes soothed them, the more she felt at sea.

Seventeen

She met him at the train station as they had arranged, and together they rode into Barcelona, where he and some other Catalán students shared an apartment. He led her past a small room with two bunk beds into a larger bedroom. His roommates weren't home. The apartment was impersonal, as if the inhabitants couldn't be caught living there. When an American student had introduced them a few nights before, at one of the bars where they socialized, she liked what she saw in his serious hazel eyes, which looked at her deeply without intruding. Then he had whispered to her and she had smiled, she had nodded, agreeing to meet him. That she barely knew him meant nothing to her. Or that his English was no better than her Spanish. Nothing mattered compared to her inner conviction. They had recognized each other and that was enough. When he knelt and sprinkled the bed with rose water, then reached across to find her, she took his hand with assurance, and helped him unhook her bra.

Eighteen

The softness of his hands belied their firmness. He could turn her over as lightly as a pillow; he stroked her legs, and they opened as if she were a cat. She was obedient to his hands as to her own impulse and soon lost the distinction, soon lost herself in arousal's persistent roar. But he kept track of her for both of them. He blew on her face and thighs to cool them; he drew her hair up and fanned it around her; he brought them fruit and chocolate and bread, and fed her, letting her also feed him. They talked as if they understood each other. She felt so attuned to him that she didn't need to distinguish all the words; his meaning had seeped into her senses, the way some poems did, the best ones, whose narratives eluded her while their music tore open her heart. She would have liked to stay forever on that bed, but he wanted to shampoo her hair.

Nineteen

After he had washed her hair twice, and sponged her body, after he had dried her with a towel, lifting her arms above her head like a child, and then wrapped the towel in a turban around her hair, after she had dressed and he had put on water for coffee, shaved, and also dressed, just as she realized in a daze that she was about to miss the last train back to school, his roommates, two boys and a girl, came home. She could see right away that the girl, who had short dark hair and bangs, and spoke heavily accented Spanish, or was it Catalán, this girl was his girlfriend. She didn't need to be told. It was one more thing she understood without needing the words, though in understanding it she upset the meaning of everything she had understood before, her damp hair and the room with damp sheets where they were now, she could hear them, rapidly interrupting each other's unfinished sentences, sentences she could not comprehend.

Twenty

In her journal later she wrote down the most rudimentary things, clues like rose water/showering/roommates. She wrote that it had been an extraordinary day, that she had thought they were soul mates, that she still hoped to hear from him. Then her pen skittered off, leaving the body of the page and tracing his long name in the margins, until it spilled over, a mantra crowding out thought. She didn't write how she had missed the train and spent the night on a bunk bed, awake and alone. How she had stared into the darkness, curled up with her hands between her legs. All night she had tried to remember what they had said to each other, what he had said, trying to capture consciously what had been intuitively received, her head aching from the effort. She would have liked to straighten out their impression of who she was. But she wasn't sure what she would say even if they shared a common reservoir of words. Spanish stymied her, but English was no easier. Her feelings were suddenly shy of words, and she was shy of her feelings. She felt bereft, deserted without resources, a person unknown even to herself. She didn't write how she hid her head under the pillow. How politely he said good-bye in the morning. How their lips had never touched.

Twenty-One

She called them back from the school's office phone. The connection delayed their voices and caused her own to echo in her ear. Her father was preoccupied, and talked about Watergate. She was proud he was on the Democratic honor roll—Nixon's enemy list. He said he'd been thinking about her on the plane, of how proud he was. Her heart began to pound. *We're both proud of you dear,* her mother chimed in. *But we wish you'd write us more about what you've been doing.* She grew quieter as her mother talked about their recent activities. Then her father interrupted. He couldn't get away, but they had decided that her mother would meet her at the end of the term and they would travel together. She tried to suppress her panic and said *Ah ha*, hoping it sounded friendly. Then she brought up her own plans for the meantime, which startled them, it was so abrupt and unexpected, as if she'd come into the room without knocking, interrupting an important conference. They disapproved. They didn't like the idea of her and her friend traveling unsupervised with two boys, and her father absolutely forbade her from going to Morocco. To this she yielded, showing reluctance and resentment in her voice, because she knew if she let him have his way on this one thing he would let her have the other, and would release the money so she could travel. She told them it was safer to travel with the boys than without them, and though in belittling their fears she risked exacerbating them, they let her go.

Twenty-Two

She was sleeping with the older brother now, she had been sleeping with the younger one before. She liked the younger one better, but now he was sleeping with her friend. The night their train from Barcelona arrived in Valencia after 2:00 A.M. all four of them slept jammed against each other, on a sofa bed in the apartment of a cab driver who had been idling near the station. It was too late to find a regular *pensión*, and he charged them very little. Although she balked at first, it suited her to be communally pressed together, as if the bond of camaraderie was stronger than their frayed sexual bond. But lying on her side, she had no room for her arms, she had to keep them above her head, and then they tingled; when she nestled them around the older brother's waist, he flung them off. So she shifted to her back, and then she shifted toward her friend, each shift setting off the bedsprings and groans and her self-conscious mortification. She hadn't thought how both brothers might dislike her until that night, one for sleeping with the other, the other because he hadn't liked her to begin with, only wanting to spite his brother and get laid.

Twenty-Three

He swore at her, and wanted her to curse him. Affection set him off. Treating her as if she were incidental to her own body, he took it over, and brushed her hands aside. When he thrust into her, the stabbing penetrated her cervix and seemed to cut into her stomach. She blanched, but tried to ride with it, to find a safe niche. Then, as suddenly as it had begun, it stopped. He pushed her away like a plate of strong cheese and wiped his mouth with the back of his hand. Her thighs burned. She must not have understood what had happened, or who he was, or who she was to him, because she wanted to talk, to tell him how she was feeling, to rest her head on his chest, as if, he said, pulling on his undershorts and sneering, as if they were in a relationship.

Twenty-Four

She leaned over the map spread out beneath the glass counter and saw the route her friend and the other two would be taking to Morocco. Granada to Gibraltar to Tangier. She would head the other way, going either to Córdoba or Sevilla, depending on which train left first. She sighed. It would be good to leave Granada. Granada was so dusty, its riverbeds dry, its gypsy caves desolate. The Alhambra had water, though, flowing water, fountains, and reflecting pools. Walking along the columns and through the archways, she had wanted to follow the sharp intricate angles of the tracery work with her finger. When she entered one of the small inner chambers, through a courtyard, she smelled the warm scent of amber and thought she heard a gurgling trickle of water and tinkling bells. Someone's charm bracelet, someone's perfume, she thought now, no longer looking at the map she leaned against, still waiting for the clerk. It would be better to leave sooner and not go back to the courtyard. It would be better to be alone, even if she didn't know what to do with herself. She sighed, not noticing the tall skinny boy to her right until he said *Excuse me* so she would move her arm and uncover Andalucía. He looked about her age, scrubbed, virginal, innocuous. She hadn't heard a Texas twang before and thought the drawl had a nice polite reticence about it, so she was friendly in turn when he asked where she was going. He was going to Córdoba, and wouldn't they both be glad of the company? Relief swarmed through her, and before she could catch herself, together with the clerk they had picked out a train.

Twenty-Five

He liked to play the guitar, and kept his fingernails long on his left hand for strumming and plucking the strings. When one of those fingers poked between her lips and touched her vulva she cringed, then gasped, as her inner flesh got snagged between finger and nail. She had known she wouldn't want him to touch her by the end of the two-hour train ride, but she didn't know how to get out of it. Not that either of them had said anything. But she'd fallen asleep and let her head slide onto his arm. He'd fingered her hair and given her a shy, satisfied smile, at which she'd flinched and lifted her head, shifting her weight, removing his hand, while keeping an eye on his smile, which didn't change. She had been too openly grateful for his company at first, so that now he took in nothing of her emotion: the further into herself she withdrew, the more of a free hand she was giving him, because she found she could not tell him, she could not find the words to tell him she'd rather he leave her alone. As if it were impolite. Instead, as he slipped his penis inside her, jiggling her hips to make her come, she prayed it was true that no experience was harmful if you learned from it, and that she would find out what it was she was supposed to learn. Then she said *Yes. I'm sure. Thank you. Could you please move now?* And left the *pensión* early in the morning before he woke. And waited at the station for a train.

Twenty-Six

The gears ground, rusty, sluggish, rasping. Heaving itself forward, teetering and swaying, the train was hardly out of the station when it halted, *thud*, against something solid, like a cow, or something imperative, mailbags left standing at the platform. At least she hadn't given him her address. Or her last name, pretending not to hear when he asked. Everyone squeezed together and popped out of the train to look around. She caught the word *hombre,* but no one who spoke Spanish simply enough knew whether the man on the tracks had been seen in time. People dawdled on the edge of the dry field and drifted back in. The conductor clanked his bell, the doors shut, the gears groaned. Each time the train lurched, her pen skidded across the page, like a stereo needle scratching an album, so she gave up working on her description of the train's jolting rhythm, its jarring noise, and promising "more later," she began leafing through the pages. At the bottom of a list of names without a heading she drew a blank line, a little sickened. It was too soon to think about. It startled her to come across scattered images, lines, flashes of poems, like shooting stars, glimpsed and recorded on occasional clear nights. Café entries always started the same way, placing herself in the café, and then confessing she didn't have anything to write about before circling very slowly toward whatever private thing it was at the center that needed to be so protectively shrouded. Working her way out, she smoothed over emotions with bravado and idealism. She wrote about exploring the uncharted territories of herself, words as seductive to her as the feel of the velvet and silk remnants she used to patch her threadbare jeans at knee or butt or thigh, and as she embroidered, her language grew more romantically colored and charged.

Twenty-Seven

At the first large intersection, the crowd from the station splintered. She started to follow the faction crossing right, but panicked midway and ran back to the curb. No new group formed to guide her. So she started off again, this time walking straight across the wide avenue. It was close to twilight. None of the squat old women wearing black dresses and black shawls, with black scarves tied around their pinned-up hair, black stockings, and sturdy black shoes would speak to her when she tried to ask them the way to town, even though in her long-sleeved leotard and cotton work pants she too was wearing predominately black. She had wanted to avoid catching any man's eye, but overhearing her, one stopped to give her directions and the address of a *pensión*. After she thanked him, she let him go ahead of her, and watched his back until he turned the corner. When she reached the *pensión*, the *duenna*, overseeing dinner and watching TV, gave her a quick look and then showed her an upstairs room facing a small courtyard. It had its own sink. She wanted to sleep but she was restless. She wasn't sure what to do with herself, so she took everything out of her small backpack, and began by rinsing and scrubbing her leotard. Now she had to stay put.

Twenty-Eight

Sunlight ricocheted off the whitewashed four-story houses. She could see bits of private courtyards behind wrought-iron gates, their fountains serenely gurgling upwards to plunge down into spirals of blue tile, the splashing loud and sweet and never-ending. Walking through Sevilla's green leafy parks, she was consciously languid, not to stretch out time, but to fill it. At the station she sat on one of the slatted benches, reading and waiting. When a train pulled in from Morocco, she quickened and sprang to life, trying to cover all the doors at once, looking for a matted braid, a blue satchel. In eighth grade they had spent all their recesses and lunch hours together, circling slowly around the playing field until the bell rang, so absorbed in each other's thoughts that they were left alone. Her friend knew how to listen; she had a deep, receptive silence that gave back as well as took in. But she also loved contagious laughter, and activity, and would cajole her until she'd agreed to go Christmas caroling or hiking or in a crowded van to the beach. She was like a long-legged pony. Only now sometimes there was a hole in the silence, vacancy, unreachable places. And she laughed for no reason. And day after day she didn't step off the train.

Twenty-Nine

She slept with the American graduate student staying in her *pensión* because he seemed nice. She slept with him because he was there. Because he asked her to. Because she didn't think it would hurt her. She slept with him after she'd seen the cathedral, the Giralda, the Alcázar, the Plaza de España, the old Jewish section; after she'd absorbed the dry heat of Sevilla's sun, daydreamed under its orange trees, and stared at its houses, in love with the whitewash, arches, grillwork, tile. She slept with him because there were hours left over. Dark hours and daylight hours. Hours after waiting for the train. Hours when she couldn't keep walking or looking or remaining amiable, impersonal, level-headed, independent. Couldn't keep making conversation with other tourists. Hours still left even after the hours when she moved from one modern café to the next, sipping her *café con leche* as slowly as she could, but not slowly enough, eating, reading, but unable to settle in, like the old men who sat from noon past sunset in the tapas bars. If only she could play cards with the old men. But men followed her as it was. Spanish men. They whispered and whistled. It made her jumpy. She knew she would have to leave soon if her friend didn't show up, but she didn't know how to get herself out, or where to go. He was nice. He was educated. When he told her to be discreet, to be quiet, that he didn't want the *duenna* to know, she was surprised at the sharp hurt, because she felt so heavily inoculated. It seemed worse to feel things this much than not to feel them at all.

Thirty

When the train to Barcelona stopped in Valencia she saw her friend sitting cross-legged on the floor of the station, resting her head against a large backpack propped against the wall. She was with a group of students from the school. One of them, soft and curly-haired, buzzed protectively around her. She saw that he had made a magic circle around her; it was clear and bright, as if drawn with thick white hopscotch chalk. She saw her friend bask in that nimbus, and that she didn't think about how the soft line enclosing her had separated them, because for her there was no line, only her all-encompassing bliss, from which she extended herself, blindly, to be embraced. But he knew the demarcation, and while he couldn't yet stop his girlfriend from reaching out, he could stop anyone else from stepping in. Just by being there. Just by nestling up beside her. They talked about Sevilla, how odd that they had missed each other, and she heard about the markets of Morocco, and the buses, and the hash, but not much about the brothers, and then she got back on her train.

Thirty-One

There was mail waiting for her at the school. Messages. That was a relief. If she hadn't been forgotten, if people wrote her letters and those letters found her, then maybe she wasn't lost, only temporarily misplaced. Maybe it would happen that one night on the verge of sleep she would reach inside herself and pull out the slender thorns lodged in her throat, womb, ovaries, the choking vines wrapped around her heart. That night she would sleep curled under a protective wing, and in the morning she would fly. But instead, reading her mail, she felt the vines tighten. Her friend from boarding school wrote how wonderful it was that she was expanding her horizons. Her boyfriend from the summer said her few letters had been so sad and vague he could tell something was wrong; he wanted her to be careful. He said he was waiting for her. And then there was a telex from her mother: Reservations confirmed. Hotel Diplomatic. Friday. May 10th.

Thirty-Two

There was time to take the train through León up to Galicia, and the bus back across to Bilbao before her mother arrived, but not enough time to diet. She had stopped smoking because of the thick green phlegm she was coughing up, but when she thought about traveling with her mother she wanted first one cigarette and then another. The school's little town bored her. It made her nervous. She had already stopped going to the bars because she still didn't know how to make conversation, she only knew how to keep to herself while waiting self-consciously for an involvement, and now she stopped going to the disco. At the disco she had liked dancing alone. Dancing, she drank only water. She was tireless. When Suzi Quatro segued into the Stones, or even the Beatles, she lost herself, ecstatic in the music. She danced as if she were an instrument essential to the song. She danced from her hips, roundly, wildly, taking as much space as she needed, exuberant, and self-involved as some musicians are, but not oblivious, never completely shutting her eyes. At first it didn't bother her that she was watched. It fed her, because she felt safe and anonymous, and she could ignore them. Then they started clustering and clucking and finally one came over. He tried to engage her eyes, to join her, to sidle up and brush against her hips, to lead her outside by the arm. She saw that having let herself go on the dance floor, she was no longer anonymous, but notorious. If she left soon, she could take the train through León up to Galicia, and the bus across to Bilbao, and still be back before her mother arrived.

Thirty-Three

He said he would drive her right to the station, but after a few minutes, they started to climb. She had thought León was flat, but the countryside was mountainous. On the side of a winding road he stopped the car. It was getting dark. He leaned toward her. She could kiss him or not kiss him, what difference did it make, as long as he drove back down? She had an idea that it was better to show him she could kiss him, and then choose not to, rather than let him think she was simply shy or cold or inexperienced. So she opened her mouth against his and let their tongues play for a second or two before she wrenched her face away and clamped her lips shut. Now her mouth tasted, like him, of rancid olive oil. Angrily, he persisted, turning her shoulders back around and taking her face in his hands, trying to prise his tongue between her teeth. She saw now that all he cared about was getting her to keep kissing him. By kissing him, she had given him a kind of permission, he must have thought, to kiss her again and again, no matter how she squinched up her lips or struggled. But at last he gave up, exasperated, disgusted. And just as she had thought it important to show him how well she could kiss before refusing him, so he made it clear, even while turning the key, that he could leave her on the mountainside at any point along the way. Her heart pounded against the gravel in her throat as they careened down. She kept her hand on the door handle and when he stopped in front of the station, she leapt out and tore through the ticket lobby, letting the bathroom door slam shut behind her.

Thirty-Four

Two *guardias civiles* lounging against the window watched her buy her ticket to La Coruña. Then they escorted her into their office. Her eyes were red from crying. She was coughing. Was she drunk? Then why had she reeled through the station? And what was she doing for so long in the bathroom? One of them looked through her passport while the other balanced a rifle on his knee. To them, she was like a lizard or a toad captured during an early evening walk. It was fun to toy with her, to probe and find out things. When they got bored they would let her go. Why would a girl her age want to travel alone? They couldn't believe her parents would even allow it. Perhaps they didn't know. Perhaps she was a runaway. Perhaps they should send a letter. Why was she so agitated? She tried not to think about their rifles; she tried not to look at their shiny black hats, which sat on the desk as if in the back room of a Mickey Mouse clubhouse. She tried to formulate plausible, neutral answers to their questions, and to concentrate on getting back her passport, now lying on the desk like a playing card.

Thirty-Five

It was Sunday. The morning had been foggy. Parents stood together behind the swings and pushed their children higher while the children howled and bayed. Couples strolled the wide promenade, arms linked, each with one hand free to pass an ice cream back and forth. There were baby strollers too, which the strolling girls, not yet engaged, snuck looks at. The sun played tag with the clouds. She sat on a bench, looking up every few sentences. Pages and pages before the end of the chapter. Unable to concentrate, she was suddenly scared about going to college. The book slid on her lap. The minutes sagged. She wondered how many times she would have to circle the park, or even La Coruña itself, to wade through all the hours. Best to sit as long as possible. To reopen the book.

Thirty-Six

The cough medicine made her drowsy. Now she could finally relax. She'd found the apartment. He was home. When he let her in, his surprise contained enough of the tone of pleasure to reassure her: she had made a good impression on him the times they'd met. He was a college student, only a little older than she, but a diplomat's son, and more sophisticated. She gave him news of the American student who had introduced them; they reminisced about the school's seaside town. She should have written to say she was coming to Bilbao. He would have had a party. What were friends for? They were friends, after all—that was a relief, though she wasn't sure what it meant. It made her want to lean harder, to take refuge. It made her crave his undiluted love. He was like an elf: playful, with none of the Spanish ferocity, no trapdoor dungeons. But lilting English, jagged bangs, a thin androgyny. In bed with him, listening to "Walk on the Wild Side," she imagined him dressed in a low-cut sequined gown and fishnets, like Lou Reed, and, suddenly carefree, began to laugh.

Thirty-Seven

It worried her. She didn't know what her mother would do when she opened the hotel room door and saw her standing there in her black work pants and black leotard, heavier than when she'd left, coughing, bedraggled, hair dirty, clothes dirty, skin, everything, smelly, dirty, and worn out, too worn out to listen to the details of her mother's first transatlantic journey alone. She was pretty sure her mother wouldn't hold her close and stroke her hair, letting her cry in her arms, before asking any questions or talking. She knew her mother would want her to bathe immediately, and would fret about her clothes, probably insisting they throw them out, but that she would not draw the bath, or test the water, or add to it a soothing oil before closing the door gently behind her. What she didn't expect, what she couldn't have known before the door opened, was the way it would feel, the sting, when she saw waves of repulsion on her mother's face. They stood one on either side of the threshold for a few seconds, neither moving until her mother composed herself, making her face a happy mask so they could both step forward to receive a kiss on the cheek and a hug.

Thirty-Eight

She didn't have much to talk about. It was awkward, with her mother watching her eat. *Spanish food is so greasy*, her mother said. *You really shouldn't have the fried potatoes.* The restaurant was nearly empty because it was the sort of place with iron grillwork and torchlights where fashionable Spaniards ate, and they ate after ten. Her mother was surprised she hadn't bought herself even a leather handbag, or shoes or boots or at least gloves. Spain was renowned for its leather. She hadn't thought of it—of buying things. Its leather and its lace and those dances. Or a bullfight. Well, her mother could understand that. But she'd been to the Prado? *Yes.* The Prado. And together they would go to the tiny Picasso museum here in Barcelona. The Picasso museum and the Sagrada Familia and the market at Las Ramblas she had remembered to tell her mother about and after two days of sightseeing they would fly first to Rome, then to Paris, then London, and, after traveling together almost an entire three weeks, together fly home. But first she had to pick up the things she'd left at the school.

Thirty-Nine

She hadn't meant to miss the train from school back to Barcelona. She certainly hadn't realized it was Mother's Day until she called her mother to tell her she'd be back in the morning. But now, with the last train gone, there was nothing she could do about it. She could sleep on a couch in the apartment some of the students had rented together. She appreciated them more now that her mother was here. And while she hadn't intended to miss the train, she hadn't wanted to leave in time to catch it. She was enjoying herself. The younger brother was telling her about Patty Hearst's transformation into Tania. The older brother had left weeks ago, and they didn't mention him. Nor did they mention her friend. They didn't talk about themselves at all, until later, when he told her that in order to get some sleep he needed to be alone. Then, in one continuous motion, he lifted himself off her, got up from the couch, and walked out of the room. She started to cry. He was leaving just as she had begun to arch her back in joy.

Forty

Waiting for the elevator after lunch, her mother stared at her. Something was wrong. Well, it had been Mother's Day. Her mother had never before dined alone in a public place. And then, she whispered in her ear, though they had the elevator to themselves, a man had propositioned her. He approached her in the lobby when she was getting her room key, but she had noticed him before, looking at her as she ordered her meal. He asked her to join him for a drink, to spend the rest of their evening together. Nothing like this had ever happened to her before, and it was upsetting, humiliating. They were in the hallway, walking to their room. She lifted her eyes to the ceiling and sighed before apologizing again. And no, she repeated impatiently once they were inside, she hadn't been visiting a boyfriend; she hadn't intended to miss the train. How many times did she have to say so. Her mother eyed her skeptically. Did she have to flirt with the bellboy? This came as a shock. What bellboy? Saturday, the one who came in with the towels, and then, just now, in the hall, she'd seen a look pass between them. Her mother was vehement, accusing. She shook her head and sat down. Three weeks of this. She picked up her journal from the table. Funny, she didn't remember, couldn't imagine, leaving it there.

Forty-One

Your what? her mother replied. *Of course not.* She wouldn't read her journal without permission. Though didn't that book she was holding in her hand say *Travel Log?* The words were embossed on the cover. It's not an itinerary, she explained, but a workbook of poems. Had she or hadn't she read it? *Of course not.* What made her think of such a thing? But she shouldn't leave it out if she didn't want people to read it. How private could it be if she left it out? She put it in her backpack where she always kept it, cursing herself, her heart still racing. How could she be so careless. She had left behind her backpack, that was bad enough, but to leave her journal out. She wouldn't have believed it if she hadn't seen it herself, lying there on the table for all the world to open and read. Finally, she decided to forget it; she didn't believe her mother would lie to her, and she'd rather think that she, of all people, as reserved as she was, would respect privacy. She'd rather not think of what she would have read. So she stopped asking, stopped suspecting, and her mother—they were checking out anyway—dropped the bellboy.

Forty-Two

The doctor who treated her for bronchitis in Rome also gave her medication for crabs. She had been itchy since leaving Córdoba, though she had stopped noticing it until, under her mother's constant scrutiny, she became conscious of scratching. She had stopped writing in her journal—she was never alone. All day they went sightseeing or shopping. Her eyes would begin glazing over in the morning, as she closed herself to the outside world, enacting like a sleepwalker her role in her mother's grand drama: Mother and Daughter Tour Europe Together Before Daughter Leaves Home for College. She couldn't deflect it; it was pointless to argue. *Why do you have to spoil everything,* her mother might say. Or, *Don't be so sensitive. That's not what I meant. Can't you be nice?* Her feelings bulldozed, she imagined the rubble being used as the foundation of an elaborate temple dedicated to the social order. So she shut herself down. Out of everything in Rome, only the Catacombs moved her. Peering into one of the ill-lit honeycombed cells, the cicerone pointed out the buried remains of a fifteen-year-old girl, a Christian martyr. She felt their kinship immediately. She knew the girl had been happy, filled with the light of her belief, though living in the dark underground. Not that it had been easy, hiding from the Roman oppressors, never seeing the sun. Perhaps this girl had also kept a record of her feelings, something no one ever saw, sacred to her as the rites. She remembered how Anne Frank's diary had both inspired and tormented her, how she had recognized herself in it, only to become confused, realizing, *But Anne wrote that, not me. Anne's the writer.* At that age she hadn't even kept a diary. And how badly she kept one now; how little she got into words; how everything inside her sank down to such a level that she could never haul it back up. . . . Her mother was calling her name. They were ready to leave. She was saying that down here it was too dark, too damp, too depressing.

Forty-Three

There's something I want to ask you. Don't get mad. She braced herself for another one of her mother's questions. They were sitting in the upstairs tearoom of WH Smith, the English bookstore on the Rue de Rivoli, near their hotel. Her mother was pouring them tea. She remembered how the night before her mother had pulled at her arm, yanking her away as she asked a man directions. It was raining and dark and they were lost, walking on the left bank after dinner. At first there was no one to be seen; the occasional taxis wouldn't stop for them. Her mother was getting more and more distraught, muttering that they shouldn't have gone walking, and clutching her to make her stay under the streetlight, when she saw the man, middle-aged and wearing a suit, walking toward them. She broke away. He spoke Spanish, not English, and listened patiently until he understood her. He offered them the cover of his umbrella while he tried to hail a cab, even as her mother dragged her into the rain. *Are you crazy,* her mother said, after giving the driver the name of their hotel. *Approaching a strange man on a dark corner on an empty street? What were you saying to him, so friendly? What kind of girl are you?* While she sat captive and mute in the car, her mother let her know again and again how upset she was. Now she was calmly squeezing the juice from a cheesecloth-covered lemon wedge. *Do you ever think about suicide?* she finally said, looking up.

Forty-Four

In London they spent an afternoon apart. By this time, she had shrunk so far into herself that she felt nothing but irritation, boredom, and claustrophobia. She acted her part, helping to choose which plays to see and where to eat, but she didn't want to go anywhere or see anything. It was an effort to breathe, an extra effort to make conversation. There was also an undercurrent of fear, as if, if she made the wrong move, her mother would take charge of her indefinitely. She knew she would gladly impose many changes if she could. She had been told since the age of twelve that when she was sixteen she could get her nose fixed, though it had never been broken. Her mother interpreted her refusal as perverse self-denial. Each time the offer was made she felt less beautiful. On this afternoon apart she wasn't feeling beautiful at all. She was feeling weighed down, heavy with inertia. It was drizzling, but she forced herself to go outside. She walked up and down the blocks near their hotel, skirting and turning back at a park. She didn't know how to free herself during this precious time; she was like a rabbit shaken out of its cage. She wanted to be alone, to scurry under a bush. Only a couple of stores interested her. At Culpeppers she bought diuretic tablets to help her lose weight. And then the luxurious smell of chocolate pulled her into a confectioner's. She bought fudge, and ate it while walking so her mother wouldn't know, eating one bite right after the other, even as she began to feel sick. It tasted so incredibly good. How could she throw it away when she normally never got any? By the time her mother got back to their room, she was already in bed, and insisted, really, that she wasn't *too* sick, but her mother should go to dinner without her. Then, finally, absolutely, safely, alone, she drifted on a delicious sea into sleep.

Forty-Five

Her father waited impatiently for them as their bags were inspected; through the plate-glass windows they could see him pacing. His hug was tight, but quick; he wanted to get going. Once they were on the freeway, she listened halfheartedly from the backseat as her mother answered questions about their trip. They had had good weather, and such a good time together, her mother insisted, she was sure neither of them would ever forget it. Her father looked at her in the rearview mirror, asking for confirmation. *Yes*, she agreed wearily, it was memorable, and *Yes,* as they pulled into their driveway, it was good to be home. Was it true? She opened the car door and got out. The smell of the eucalyptus trees lining their drive cleared her head, made room for the idea that it might be.

Forty-Six

The graduation ceremony was in the afternoon, on the lawn outside the main building. Shopping with her mother, she had found a loose, knee-length, brown dress to wear. Her mother had argued that it was too drab, but she thought it hid her weight and insisted on getting it. Now she saw that some of her classmates, like the knowing girl with whom she used to read Neruda, had on tight, strapless evening gowns. The audience faced into the parched hills that rose above the dormitories, while the graduating class faced their parents and the school behind them, the asphalt paths shimmering in the heat. During the headmaster's speech, two naked boys flew by on a ridge, hooting and waving. Some parents laughed, some gasped. Hers seemed not to have seen them, focused as they were on the headmaster's homilies. Later, dressed in shorts, the two boys accepted their diplomas with the rest of the class. There were only about thirty students, but she felt as if no one noticed her, noticed she was back, or that she'd been away. Earlier, on the phone, the girl had nonchalantly agreed—it did seem obvious now—that, sure, adventures could be shallow, disappointing, even disheartening, but even so she stopped herself from saying how wretched she was feeling. She didn't want anyone to know just how low she felt, since it didn't seem to show, and, besides, she didn't ascribe the feeling to anything in particular. After the presentation of diplomas, she accepted her parents' congratulations with what she hoped was the proper enthusiasm and kissed them good-bye. The entire graduating class was staying in the dorms one last night; that evening, back in her leotard and work pants, she snuck onto the library deck with everyone else and toked on a cone-shaped jay, a spliff, somebody called it, that made them giddy even before it got them high.

Forty-Seven

Of all the things her father let her know when he called her into his den the next evening to tell her how upset they were over what her mother had read in her journal—their deep distress and disgust, such a feeling of revulsion he could barely face her, let alone want to kiss or hug her, so that he had considered kicking her out and casting her off, though after wrestling with his feelings he had decided against it, maybe against his better judgment, but out of love, and a feeling of responsibility; he could never live with himself always wondering what had happened to her, not knowing how she was, he had such fears for her; he worried, he had to tell her, that if she wasn't careful, and didn't limit herself to sleeping with two, well, maybe three, boys while she was at college, she would get a reputation, and she'd already made it more difficult for herself to find a man she could marry, she would have to find someone unusual, he would have to be very unusual; it hurt him more than she'd ever know, that she had broken her word, she had promised, didn't she remember he'd made her promise, she wasn't going to be sexually active at boarding school, not until college, like her sister; he would never have let her go without that promise, he should never have let her go, her mother was against it, that horrible wild place, she should have stayed home and gone to Catholic girls' school, but he hadn't wanted to force her, he had respected her, had trusted her, and look what she had done, he was livid, she had broken her word, she had defiled herself, didn't she have any morals, any self-respect, she had betrayed them, they wracked their brains but couldn't figure out what they had done wrong, they had always loved her, she had always been loved, how could she have done such awful things, he hadn't realized she was so immature, she would regret it all, she would see, he was sure, she would regret everything she had done, when she realized what it meant, it broke his heart—of all these things, reiterated and elaborated while she sat silent on the couch, stony-faced and unrepentant, she wanted to pursue only something he had almost passed over, and she clung to it as long as she could, dismissing as irrelevant everything else. Her mother had read her journal. Her mother had read her private journal without permission and then denied it, lying to her; had traveled with her for three weeks, treating her like a leper but pretending, insisting, that nothing was wrong; and then, when they finally got home, had not even told her herself, but had turned the whole matter over to her father, because she knew she had done something unforgivable, that she would never be forgiven.

Forty-Eight

Later, she would tell everyone she talked to what her mother had done. But at first, that night, she felt like a prisoner of war, isolated deep within the impenetrable heart of an enemy encampment. She had no diversions, no lines in or out, no stereo, no telephone, no radio, no car. Her sister, who might or might not have understood, was away. At least, with the door shut, she could cry freely. She never wanted to open her journal again, though she knew that eventually she would have to. She would have to learn to write without seeing the shadow of her mother's face on the page, and her father's looming behind that. In her bathroom, in the farthest recess of her room, she pressed a towel into the crack at the bottom of the closed door and opened the window, hoping she wouldn't set off the burglar alarm. The lit match hissed as it hit the water in the toilet bowl. Exhaling through the fine mesh screen into the dark, cricket-sentried night, she wondered if her parents would ever let her go, and how she would manage in the new world.

Forty-Nine

The next day when she was called into the den, she remained standing by the door. Her mother was also there. She glared at her, but otherwise was careful not to let any of her emotions show. It was too dangerous. Her mother called her by name, beseeching her, but her feeling of righteousness was a protective shield. They would not find out anything they did not already know. Her mother delicately cleared her throat. She had something to say. Of course she hadn't realized what it was when she picked it up, and she hadn't read most of it, she hadn't read much at all, but that was beside the point. The point was that the little she had read had been enough to alert her that something was terribly wrong, which she had sensed in any case the minute she opened the hotel room door in Barcelona. What she was trying to say was that she really had to understand the position that she, as her mother, was in. Someday she would understand. But for now all her mother asked, the only thing they would insist upon, was that she do them this one favor and talk to a man they knew, a counselor whose specialty happened to be sex. *It's obvious,* her father interrupted from behind his desk, *that we can't talk to you about this rationally, and we want you to talk to someone who can.* She was oddly embarrassed, wondering how her parents had come to know a sex counselor, but she nodded and said she would go.

Fifty

She believed him when he said he would not judge her; that he was only concerned with her well-being, with how she felt about herself and her actions. He had a large corner office with windows all along two sides. She could see her mother's Mercedes in the parking lot, and behind it she could see the hills across the road. Driving the Mercedes always made her cringe, and they talked about that too. He complimented her vocabulary—he had been impressed with her use of the word *exacerbate*, a word she had always liked but never found herself remarkable for using. His comment made her feel secretly proud, the more sophisticated of the two. Since he smoked a pipe, she felt free to smoke her cigarettes—and she somehow trusted that he would not tell her parents, that he would not tell them anything. But still there were things she could not bring herself to say. It was too embarrassing to talk about sexual details. She didn't like talking about sex at all, except to make it clear that she had no feelings of guilt, that she considered her body her own to do with as she wished. But did she know what it was she wished, he would ask her, and she would cry, trying to sort it out. It took all summer to persuade her that she had left out her journal because she unconsciously wanted her mother to read it, though she never could figure out why. Neither of them considered the possibility that she later came to think more likely—that she hadn't left it out at all, but that her mother had foraged in her backpack, and then left the journal on the table, signaling it had been read.

Fifty-One

She cupped her hands under her breasts and held them up so that they were high and firm, like the rounded breasts of an Indian goddess. She hadn't seen herself in a full-length mirror for a long time. Her nipples were coral colored. Her stomach and hips had developed curves, because of the extra weight. She knew that underneath she had narrow, almost straight hips, but still it didn't look so bad. She wondered who she was, inside the flesh, and whether she was still the skinny lithe girl who used to sit reading and dreaming for hours in the branches of an oak tree, or if this soft round creature had swallowed her. She wondered who she was going to become, and wished she were back in the branches of that tree, in the hills behind their old house. She wanted to lean into the generous arms of that wide full oak and close her eyes and smell sweet dried grass and old cow dung. First she would climb the fence separating their yard from the untended vegetable garden, and then slip through the gap in the barbed wire. In her dreams, the cows always got through the barbed wire, and through the fence, into the yard. They swam in the pool. The cows swam happily in the pool, and she swished the tall grass with her hand. She stepped closer to the mirror and stared until she finally saw herself not as a stranger, but with her own familiar eyes. It was time to make peace. She could feel the foxtails, the stickles, clinging to her socks and pricking her ankles. She climbed the tree and rubbed her shins against the rough bark, then circled the branch with her arms. Lying on her stomach, she hugged the tree with all four limbs. She let her body sink into it. She tightened her embrace. She'd sleep there like a leopard. The tree was her true love and she'd never let go. The tree was her mother, and would always open its lap to her, always extend its arms. Once she had found a cow skull on the other side of the hill. Once a boy had kissed her there.

Part Two

"Once more! this is a story of education, not of adventure! . . . What one knows is, in youth, of little moment; they know enough who know how to learn."

—*The Education of Henry Adams*

One

Her roommates hadn't arrived yet, so the first thing she did after lugging her old camp trunk and new Smith Corona electric up five flights of stairs was to go back down and sit in the sun, pen and notebook in hand. Her dorm was in a grassy quadrangle lined with other freshman dorms and crisscrossed by paths. Anyone could stroll through the archways that separated the college's "yard" from the town's "square" of commercial streets, but only on certain weekends were the large, wrought-iron gates swung wide. As at a tailgate party, all around her were open station wagons, but instead of picnic baskets and portable radios, they spilled suitcases and loose speaker wires tangled in lacrosse sticks. Her own parents were home in California: she had insisted on flying across the country by herself, and spent a week visiting her sister at college in Connecticut before taking the four-hour bus ride to Boston, and from the bus station a cab. She had grown used to buses in Spain, but the cab ride along the river, the sun sparkling on the water, glinting off sails and newly waxed oars, dazzled her. She wondered how long it would take her to acclimatize. Warming up in the late afternoon sun with her eyes closed, she heard the soft insinuation of someone sitting down on the grass beside her. Not a fellow student, it turned out, but a grown man in a lumber jacket, just, he said, passing through. Whatever it was that led her to guide him up the stairs of her dorm, his pressure on her shoulder or her pride, a secret pleasure she'd come to take in flouting taboo, when, dazed and disheveled, they emerged from her small room with its single bed, oak desk, and unpacked trunk a lead weight on the floor, she found that her two roommates, in the short time it took for him to come in her mouth, had arrived, and were examining the college's insignia on their desk chairs, waiting to meet her.

Two

Just as she skipped her freshman mixer because her parents had met at theirs, so she decided in advance that she couldn't major in English because her mother had, and she couldn't recall ever seeing her mother read a book. Magazines, yes, but not books, even though there was a partial shelf in their den, a gilded ghetto, as her parents used to call certain towns on the East Coast, of books from a poetry class her mother had taken. A gilded ghetto, but a ghetto nonetheless, a ghost town, herself the only visitor. In the Untermeyer anthology, as much as the poems themselves, she had pored over cribs in her mother's even hand explaining a poem's encoded meaning, its contextual place in the canon. But it was obvious her mother had retained none of it, had forgotten altogether patterned griefs, snowy woods, and rolled trousers, and the fear that she too would forget these things made her skittish. Now the course catalog, thick and squat, lay inert in her hands. She couldn't decide what to take. Finally, her roommates, a premed student and a historian's daughter, helped her puzzle it out like a Baedeker, signing her up for intro to philosophy, a soc-sci course, astronomy to get her science over with, and, what all freshmen had to take, expository writing.

Three

She noticed him right away. For one thing, he was tall; for another, he was one of the few boys with long unruly hair, dirty blond hair that hung in loose corkscrews down his neck. She didn't know when she had decided only a boy could truly understand her. It was an assumption she had picked up early, like the assumption that she would go to college. Perhaps it came from fairy tales, *Snow White* to *Barbarella*. She didn't question it, but only wondered, walking out of Mem Hall after orientation, what it would be like to have a real boyfriend, to hold hands and be monogamous. Hadn't this been what she'd always intended? Catching up with him, she touched his arm and asked to bum a cigarette, even though she had stopped smoking, and could tell by the sickly sweet smell that they were menthols. He was from New York, from one of those schools whose names she was becoming familiar with, but the nuances of which she hadn't mastered. At Mug and Muffin, he talked about Eliot, on whom he'd written his senior thesis. Her coffee at her lips, she looked up at him with stark admiration. She'd never heard of high school senior theses, and she'd never met a boy who talked about poetry. She'd also never heard of his mother, a syndicated columnist. This last assertion he found suspect, but she could see it would be in her favor, if he could only believe it. On the way back to his room, at the kiosk, she bought a pack of her own, menthols, for a change.

Four

On the thrift-shop couch he and his roommates had bought, he reached past her for matches and then kissed her on the way up, at the same time slipping the matchbook inside the cellophane of his pack. It wasn't clear whether the matches were a ploy or the kiss an afterthought; he seemed to want both. With his free hand in her hair, his breath in her ear, he led her down the hall to a room almost entirely filled by a bunk bed. The walls were so close, he could—did— kick the door shut after he sat down, though when they heard voices in the outer room he had to get up to lock it. It was a relief that he was sexually confident; she had been nervous about appearing more experienced than he; she didn't want to be the one who knew what to do. She liked to be led to a place where she felt safe enough to be wholehearted. As his hands ran their course over her body, neither skimming nor snagging, she remembered with rapture that he played the piano. Whorls into whirlpools, his mouth and hands drew her down until she couldn't do without him, she had to draw him in. Their crescendo was long, it was matchless; it reminded her that yearning was more than a wound to be staunched, that desire was a prelude, pleasure its natural fulfillment. They lay for a long time collapsed together before he lit them both a cigarette. Blowing out smoke, he wanted to gossip about their pasts, but she laughed him off, saying, *I never kept track, until you.*

Five

Walking into the Union, where all the freshmen ate, she was flayed by shyness. Day by day, she vacillated: was it better to come early and sit down alone and see who, if anyone, would join you, or better to come late when the tables were crowded and pick a group to join, a group whose members might or might not look up and nod as you sat down? Either way, after leaving your jacket in the cloakroom, you had to stand in the hot-food line and make conversation or look down at your feet. When you reached the end of the salad bar you were faced with a gauntlet of aisles between long tables. Walking to a seat, you felt watched and ignored at the same time. Three rooms to choose from, but if you passed through one, you could not change your mind and go back: it was too gauche, too embarrassing; it said, I choose you only after finding no one better, or it said, no one else will have me. Many freshmen protected themselves by arriving in packs, herds, and flocks, and theoretically she could join the drove from her dorm, but she didn't want to belong with them, and they instinctively thought her snobby and, except for her roommates, didn't include her. She spooned bacon bits onto her salad and held her tray in front of her, not like a shield, but like a chalice, full to the brim, requiring balance in every step.

Six

Not all the dorms were coed, since there were almost twice as many boys in the freshman class as girls, but hers was, with girls and boys on alternating floors. Each floor had its own common but single-sex bathroom, and if you wanted to get a rise out of someone you had only to bring up the idea of boys in T-shirts and jockeys and girls in flannel nightgowns brushing their teeth side-by-side. Because she had begun to identify herself as a feminist she always argued for it, but privately the thought made her uncomfortable. One day, walking up the stairwell, she'd had to slap a boy who, as he passed her on his way down, looked straight at her sweatered breasts and said loudly to another boy, *Speaking of stacks*. It was a good, resounding slap that surprised her as much as it did him, and she thought it at least as justified as the first one she'd given, to her mother just last summer, after overhearing herself called a whore. But her dormmates—even the girls, she realized from the frosty way they nodded when she said hello—considered the action outré, identifying with his sense of outrage, not hers. Only one girl, a lank-haired Classics major, clucked sympathetically, absentmindedly listening to the story as she ripped open packets of sugar with inky fingers and dipped her tongue in like a hummingbird, eventually picking the moistened paper apart and eating that too.

Seven

He and his roommates were trying out for the humor magazine, and regarded making puns while watching game shows as part of their training. They were all clever, and competitive. She felt more confident in bed than out of it. Sitting with them on their thrift-shop furniture during *Jeopardy*, she might as well have been a transfer student from a junior college in Hoboken, she felt so outfoxed. Even had she been from Hoboken, they couldn't have ignored her more, looking her way only as they slid another menthol from her pack on the crate that served as a coffee table. She consoled herself by remembering that only minutes before he and she had been whispering intimacies as they lounged and lunged, playful as dolphins, finally lying side-by-side, flexing their feet on the bedsprings of the upper bunk as they teased and probed. She liked the close quarters, the containment, of the bunk bed: it reminded her of those stars whose energy became denser as they compacted. A thought for her journal, or—he was taking astronomy too—a thought to tell him? Although it was the one class in which she could use the help, they never studied or sat together. Sometimes they'd have coffee afterwards or, more often, go to his room, locking his bunkmate out. She decided she'd better scribble the image down before she forgot it, but afraid one of them would notice, swoop it out of her hands, read it aloud, and use it as fodder for a parody, making the magazine on the back of her verse, she feigned an overdue paper and fled.

Eight

Restless after studying, she headed toward the River Houses, only to circle back up again. She thought that Bow Street, curved, and bumpy with cobblestones, could be an alley in Barcelona. The cobbles dug into her soles. Spain was not something she usually thought about; she only flirted with remembering. She had vowed once never to feel shame, shame was too shameful to let oneself feel, too fraught with unexamined mores, but there it was, along with an unaccountable fear, cordoning her off. The cobbles pocked and stung. Though the fall air was clear and still, she pulled her jacket tighter, bunching up the front buttons. The past, she thought, was like malaria: inside you always, able without warning to reduce your entire self to shivers and shakes, to delirium. The travel slides in her head were out of order and going too fast. She didn't want images of herself naked pasted to the lampposts. Who had control of the clicker—her feet, hurrying over the cobbles? Hearing laughter, she realized she'd been muttering to herself, nodding *sí* and shaking *no*, shrugging *quizás* and lifting her hands *no sé* in pantomimed Spanish. When she heard someone call her name, at first she thought it was inside her head, but then she heard it a second time. In English, coming from Pamplona, a little café below street level—it was a girl from her soc-sci class, at a table crowded with students. Spooning her café au lait, she sat quietly as the talk of others slowly filtered its way in.

Nine

From wedge sandals when she first arrived to leather boots as the leaves crimped and dropped in the chill air, no matter which shoes she wore, they always squeaked on the library's linoleum. Scanning titles, she craved books, but after twenty pages of the assigned hundred, she would catch herself daydreaming, whether over Max Weber or Plato. The air was stuffy, the brick building a mausoleum. She missed the olive trees of Spain, the apricot orchards of home, roads that wound across and over hills, through patches of mist, down into pumpkin fields and then north and south along the ocean. She missed history manifest in the cool white of mission churches. She wanted to be cool herself, thin, to wear, like one girl, a man's oversized white cotton shirt with the cuffs rolled halfway up her forearms and the tail hanging out. She wanted a friend, like that girl in the oversized shirt, who knew her beyond explaining. She wanted, if she closed her eyes in order to feel the essence of herself, to open them on someone, a boy with whom, after making love, to discuss the idea of essences. She remembered the time in high school she lay buoyant in a sensory-deprivation tank and felt everything that she thought mattered slide away, like the prisoner released from Plato's cave, whose soul "suffered a conversion toward the things that are real and true." She wanted to tell someone about it, but, even if it were possible to whisper in the library without a loud hissing echo, she had no one to whisper to, so she began her expos paper, due the next day, with a description of how stepping into the salt-water tank she had stepped out of the self she knew. She guessed that her teacher, a law student with the imagination of a burrowed turnip, would be baffled by it, but she never wrote for him, she wrote only for herself.

Ten

It couldn't have been more hilarious, a boy from her dorm was telling her as they walked out together. *It couldn't have been more perfect. It was like you were Barbara Stanwyck when you slapped him on the stairs.* It still enflamed her to remember the other freshman's archness at her expense; she was heartened that someone had been amused by the incident, but also distressed that it was remembered. The boy at her side was from Teaneck, New Jersey, skinny with black curly hair down past his shoulders. Half Italian, half Irish, he kept his hair in a ponytail, tucked his jeans into tan leather calf-high boots, wrote his papers in neat block handwriting, and deconstructed the lecheries of New York rocker-poets as if he were an oral historian of sex. They had recently taken to hanging out. That he was gay but used to sleep with his best friend from home, a woman who had consorted with both Bob Dylan and Patti Smith, was tantalizing—if unverifiable.

Eleven

After dinner one night, leaving her coat hanging in the Union's cloakroom where she'd managed, at the height of the rush, to uncover an empty hook, she trudged upstairs to an introductory meeting for *The Independent,* the student weekly. It was one of the first cold nights, and her coat was new: floor-length, dark brown, tucked at the waist, the only piece of clothing, aside from a pair of overalls her roommate had given her, that she was passionate about. She wasn't bold or committed enough to try out for the daily *Crimson,* with its rigorous selection process, its machismo politics, but she liked the idea of working as a writer, if not the idea of news. She'd read Tom Wolfe, Hunter Thompson, and Joan Didion; they were her heroes, along with e.e. cummings, Sylvia Plath, and Robinson Jeffers. She had to start somewhere, to find a place for herself. So she trudged up the wide, echoing steps, listened to the introduction, got an assignment to cover a meeting of a women's self-help group, and trudged back down, remembering the coat only as a blade of cold air slashed through the seam in the double doors and brandished its way down the hall. Her coat, however, wasn't there. The hooks, earlier hidden by overlapping layers of parkas, peacoats, shearlings, and scarves, now gleamed in position, like the brass section of a miniature orchestra, row after row curving upward and empty, except for one crimson windbreaker and one collapsible umbrella, the kind bought curbside in New York for a dollar, or five, if, like now, it had begun to rain.

Twelve

She saw him leaning in the doorway as she was talking to her parents on the phone, so she told them he was waiting for her. She was glad to have an excuse to end their weekly phone call; they never let her get off easily. Watching his eyes narrow as she began to answer her father's questions—coffee, New York, the first week, astronomy, very nice—she deliberately made neither too much nor too little of him. He seemed to relax and be, in an ironic, bemused way, pleased. An hour later, coming up the Algiers's basement steps, he confided that had she started telling her parents who his mother was, he would have walked out. But she hadn't even mentioned his last name, she protested, it never occurred to her. *I know,* he said, giving her shoulder a nudge. They had stopped in an alcove. Scanning the window, she saw a pair of earrings she liked—gold hoops, hand-hammered, sharp-edged, oval—and looked up excitedly. *Yes,* he agreed, *they're nice, but don't expect me to buy them.*

Thirteen

As a woman in the center of the circle waved a plastic speculum in the air and explained that it worked by widening the vaginal walls so it was possible to see up into the cervix, a second woman, slouched in a chair with her skirt hiked and her legs apart, demonstrated, parting her lips with one hand and sliding the instrument up with the other. Though, it was emphasized, no two vaginas were alike, a healthy cervix was rosy, and higher up, open at ovulation, lower and closed at menses. With the speculum now inserted, the woman in the chair showed how to tilt a hand mirror to see inside, and invited everyone to come look. Though she demurred, she felt unexpectedly at home in the setting: it reminded her of sitting around a wood fire at girls' camp. Songs she'd sung there, like "Kumbaya" and "The Cat Came Back," were often in her head. She wondered if her parents realized, as she recently had, that the two women who ran the camp were a lesbian couple. *Lesbian couple.* The idea, the words, were new. Would they have let her go there if they'd known? Would they have let her go even to this college had they known that she would attend meetings like this one, where she was invited to look up an upperclasswoman's vagina? How like Scylla and Charybdis to them would be the choice between unchecked heterosexuality and any kind of lesbianism. For wouldn't looking up another woman's vagina be interpreted as lesbianism? Smiling to herself, she took her new speculum back to her dorm room and wrote up a simplified, modest account, her first and last for *The Independent.*

Fourteen

First he refused to tell her whether he'd slept with an old friend over the long weekend. Then he stung her by repeating what his academic advisor had offered in passing: *No one ended up with his freshman girlfriend.* It was their first fight. She didn't need to consult her advisor whom, in fact, she hadn't seen since orientation, when he had dissuaded her from taking Latin. She could reason for herself: some things you had to give up. Just as, no matter how much she liked chocolate cheesecake, she didn't want to spend her whole life neurotically losing and gaining the same ten pounds, so, no matter how much she liked him, she didn't want to spend her days and nights agonizing over whether he was faithful. Cheating on someone was different from being alone and sleeping around. It was the difference between breaking a promise and not making one. He shrugged. It was her decision. Her eyes welling over, the plaid camp blanket she'd lent him rolled up under her arm, she gave him one last kiss. Up close, she thought she could detect in his eyes little flecks of regret, but then, like cinnamon dust folded into the foam of a cappuccino, they sank and dissolved into relief.

Fifteen

At the party, standing around the piano over drinks, he said he recognized her from soc-sci. She took that as a compliment; over two hundred people attended the biweekly lectures and she had never noticed him. Now they were catty-corner, his back blocking her from the rest of the room, and she had nothing to do but memorize his tousled looks, which gave him the air of having just gotten in from walking on a windy beach, or just out of bed. Most everyone there was, like him, an upperclassman. Her roommate had cajoled her into going, but then found a group from the radio station to talk with. Uncomfortable, nervous, she had hovered near them until he saved her. It still made her feel special to be singled out. But in his bed, with his hands on her shoulders pushing her down under the grimy sheets and pinning her there, she was reminded how common desire was, how common it could make you feel if you were only its tool. It was too familiar a sensation, too familiar to ignore. How many times a year do college boys change their sheets, she wondered, trying to make light of it to herself, trying to concoct a joke as pithy as *how many coeds does it take . . . ?* But it wasn't a good joke, and she was its punch line, its butt, until he let go of her shoulders and she threw the covers off, gasping for air.

Sixteen

The hallways in the psychiatrist's building were lined with black plastic, the floors covered with loose sheets of plywood, the elevators out of order. Walking up the twisting service stairs, turning sharp corners to find his office, discombobulated her; by the time she sat down in the vestibule, she couldn't remember why she'd made the appointment. With an old-fashioned goatee and red bow tie, he looked stern and professorial, nothing like her therapist of last summer. Staring past him, she found a collection of African masks staring back, flanked by shields and spears. They started out cautiously, civilly, until she gradually found herself telling him about walking down Bow Street and the memories that had assailed her, but not about the upperclassman. When she was done, and he leaned forward in his chair, summarizing in his own language what he'd heard, it turned out there were two words she couldn't abide, especially when applied to her by a steely older man: *promiscuous* and *privileged*. The words were like arrows dipped in curare: the sting of truth nothing compared to the piercing pain of judgment. Squirming in her seat as if tied to it, she didn't give in: the words, she insisted, were tainted, implying a judgment she could infer he made by choosing them. No, he retorted, they were innocuous, neutral, factual; it was she who tinged them—why did they make her uncomfortable, defensive? With that, for a small sum payable at once, he released her. Furious at his denial, she bolted through the twists and turns, bursting simultaneously onto the street, into tears.

Seventeen

On the way up or down from her room, she usually avoided looking in the door of the boy she had slapped, which was almost always open, but tonight there was loud music, and voices shouting to be heard over it, a keg of beer on the landing. She hesitated. Was it only she who hadn't been told about the party? Did they despise her that much? She couldn't help poking her head in, and when the boy from Teaneck grabbed her hand and dragged her into the middle of the room, she didn't resist. But not until they were really dancing, whirling and gyrating, did her sense of grievance dissipate, flowing into the words of the songs they mimed: *Heart-brea-ker . . . I say I need a man; you say maybe you can.* She flung her arms in the air, flexed her hands like a cat kneading a cushion. His hands on her hips rotated them toward his own, slowly, as if coaxing. *Stop.* They put their palms out flat like traffic police. *Think it o-o-ver.* His index finger wagged in the air, exaggerating the words, emphasizing the beat. She liked that they were making a spectacle of themselves, that they were camp, that everyone was watching. It fed her feeling that she knew things they could only dream of. The boy she had slapped raised his beer to her and she allowed him a thin, icy smile, as if, in her world, she were host and he the gatecrasher.

Eighteen

As soon as she entered the lecture hall, she saw the upperclassman, sitting next to the aisle two thirds of the way back, chatting with friends. Whatever it was that connected her to him, so that, like a magnetized orb, her eye pivoted exactly to where he was, she wanted to be rid of, to spit it out of her system like snake venom, as she'd seen gypsy women in Granada do. To spit, even, in his face. Clutching her notebooks to her chest, she intended to walk right by him, so indifferent as to be ignorant of his presence. As she made her way up the steps, she avoided looking at him, busying herself by looking this way and that for someone she knew to sit with. At the last second, just as she was passing him, she stumbled on a riser, and putting her hand on his armrest to right herself, looked up into his wink.

Nineteen

When one of the self-help organizers she'd interviewed invited her to join a consciousness-raising group, she felt as though she'd been offered entrance into the Eleusinian Mysteries. The five other women were juniors, and though they seemed to her more at ease with life, they framed their crises the same way: boyfriends, parents, roommates, schoolwork. One of them was even a poet, who wore silver Hand of Fatima earrings and black cotton Chinese flats she said you could get at Woolworth's, and who wrote so persuasively about hitchhiking in New Jersey with a knife strapped to her thigh you could almost imagine she'd done it. Listening to her talk about the *good boyfriend*, on his way out, versus the *bad*, already on his way in, mesmerized her. Reading the poems, she saw herself walking near Córdoba early one morning, farmhouse cheese in her backpack, cars slowing to catcall, and wondered what stopped her from writing about it, from turning herself into a mythic heroine, a Jack—Jacqueline—Kerouac. When she read in one poem of a sky "promiscuous with stars," the image, reminding her of the swirling blues and yellows, the piercing steeple, in the van Gogh poster she had above her bed at home, gave her a small, thrilling chill: the redemption of a word she had thought irredeemable. For days it reverberated in her throat, pinked her wrist.

Twenty

She was intensely gratified that her expos teacher couldn't make heads or tails of the cummings poem she had used as an epigraph— "silence // .is / a / looking // bird:the // turn / ing;edge, of / life // (inquiry before snow." Reading his comments as she walked across the yard back to her dorm, she flipped through the pages quickly. As she had predicted, he didn't understand why being in the sensory deprivation tank and having every certainty slip away made her feel "so high." That was gratifying, too. Then she looked for the booby trap she had planted in the middle of the paper, a poem of her own, that began: "I am an empty skull / Full of empty air" and ended ten lines later, "Filled with visions / Waiting for rebirth." That it turned out he found the poem "too bleak to love" but "great poetry—you describe the indescribable rather well" was so disturbing she stopped in the middle of the path, letting backpacks and book bags swing into her as students rushed by on their way to class. It was no victory that he, baffled by cummings and bound by convention, found her poem great. It was like having someone whose lipstick matched her sweater admiring your new boots, it made you want to throw them into the back of the closet to fill up with spiders; but, insipid man, if he was sympathetic to her, how could she maintain her mocking stance?

Twenty-One

She could maintain her mocking stance, the poet asserted, because she was not beholden to anyone. Not to her admirers, her detractors, her employers, her teachers. Not to the people who paid her rent or whom she paid rent to. Not her parents. Not her friends. *You are beholden only to the truth.* The poet took a bite of bagel and gave her a hard look, to make sure her words had penetrated. A member of SDS in its waning days, she found it natural to mix motherly advice with a good diatribe. The C-R group had fallen apart over midterms; they were having lunch at the river house where the poet lived. Sitting off to one side together, she found the large raucous dining hall cozy and friendly. People stopped by to say hello as they returned their trays, or waved from across the room. Someone, the *bad* boyfriend, it was later confirmed, pinched the poet's shoulder as he sauntered by. Out of desperation, she'd given the poet a packet of her own work to read; the poet was saying it was as good as any in the beginning workshops—a comment that managed to encourage and deflate her at the same time—when, a little sheepishly, as if he knew he shouldn't, a large stocky boy sat down to join them. It was the *good* boyfriend, now no boyfriend at all, just, just what—an admirer, a detractor? Still disconcerted by the assessment of her poems, annoyed at the interruption, she gave him a wide, dissembling smile when he set his coffee down, wider than she'd meant to. Glancing at the poet as if to ask *What do we do now?*, she was embarrassed to catch them in a private joke: he swatting her hand away as she tried to poke him in the ribs.

Twenty-Two

With an orange leotard, he drew stares as he walked through the Union, and low murmured jeers, too soft to carry above the din, but spreading like a fungus just below it. Still, he would saunter in, as though equally oblivious to the attention he soaked up as to the derision he shrugged off. She never said so aloud, but she admired his cool. When, sitting not quite directly across from each other, they started talking at lunch one day, it came out that he wrote poetry. And, despite all the snickers, had a girlfriend—which didn't stop him from inviting her to his room to *share poems*, or her from saying yes. But it really must be *her* room, she thought hazily, propped on her elbow on the futon, eye level with a row of wedges, heels, boots, and fuzzy slippers lining one wall. As they passed poems and a jay back and forth, she found herself determining which shoes she would keep and which discard, had they been hers. She particularly admired a pair of black suede stack-heeled boots. How could the same girl own bunny slippers, she wondered, as he lazily slid his hand up and down her arm, telling her that he and his girlfriend had an agreement about *extra friends* before finally lowering her bra strap and turning to kiss the smoke off her mouth. How pleasant an arrangement, she thought, taking him at his word. With their clothes piled on the floor, she stopped imagining herself in the other girl's shoes; it was enough to borrow her boyfriend.

Twenty-Three

She would never admit that her father's warning rang in her ears. One of the things she liked about college was how easy it was to pretend parents didn't exist. But sometimes, standing in the shower, or sorting through reading notes, trying to decipher her own handwriting, she would catch herself arguing with him. She could sleep with whomever she wanted, she told the harsh spray pelting her face; there was no reason to keep count and ration lovers like calories. What did he know about the pleasures of having your head float away from your body as the sky swallowed you? He knew how to respect and wield authority, but not how to reject it. He hadn't grown up intrigued by circles of hand-holding, blissed-out souls swaying in unison on the public library's lawn; he wasn't reared on footage of a young girl trying to outrun the napalm consuming her body. She may have been a child in the sixties, but she was also a child *of* the sixties. Which generation was better off, her father's, that tabooed sex, or hers, that tabooed money? For an obsession, she would choose sex over money any day.

Twenty-Four

Having been taught by her mother to ask men about their interests, but not their motives, when she finally went to the science center one morning to get help with astronomy from her section leader, she found out where he had been an undergraduate (City College), what the great observatories were (Palomar, Mount Wilson, Mauna Kea), and where he'd like to end up teaching (City College), but not whether the two paper cups and bottle of whiskey he pulled out of his desk drawer were in celebration of her new comprehension of thermodynamics, simply his habit at the end of office hours, or a special exception made in honor of her visit. At first it seemed harmless enough to sip and chat, dutifully nodding as he vented his disaffection from the powers that be. Nasal and wiry, he seemed harmless as a terrier. Only when he climbed onto the desk to sit on the edge nearest her, and then leaned in to pull her close as he hooked his feet into the arms of her chair, did she remember that terriers were used to drive game out of their burrows, and realize the magnitude of her mistake.

Twenty-Five

What did you expect? Her mother's voice, sharp with reproach, sounded through the pillow jammed into her ear. *Do you think he'd treat a nice girl like that? Drinking whiskey in the morning. What kind of message do you think that sends? Haven't you learned anything?* She had been in bed since dinner, curled up tight as a fern frond. Neither her blanket nor her heartbeat reverberating in her ribcage like timpani could muffle the over-enunciated words. Her mouth filled with the taste of rancid olive oil, her nose with the smell of strong cheese. Where had she been, in the middle of one night, peeing into a tin cup? Valencia? Córdoba? *You don't understand anything,* she finally answered, turning on her other side, her back to the room as if her mother were really in it. It could have been worse. It could have been a lot worse. His office door could have been locked. He could have flipped her over onto the desk. Instead, like a contortionist, she had slithered out of his grasp, shimmying feet-first out the side of the chair. She hadn't had to knee him or throw whiskey in his face, or suffer through it. Her nervous laughter had stung, though, she could see that in his eyes, which suddenly went soft with hurt. When he took his glasses off to clean them it was all she could do to keep herself from apologizing, he looked so forlorn. *Can I call you?* he had asked, but already halfway out the door, she pretended not to hear.

Twenty-Six

The cotton raincoat she had borrowed from a girl in her dorm had a flannel lining. She liked the way, two sizes too big, it wrapped around her like a cocoon; with a bulky sweater under it, she could stay warm enough to pupate through winter. No one, not even she, could tell what would emerge, moth or butterfly. She wasn't used to the crunch of fresh snow under her boots, or the slog of melting slush. The stillness of snowfall, bare black branches crusted over with white, increased her melancholy like the tremor of a violin's last note, the curtain sweeping shut on a tableaux of dancers, tutus tilted up as they leaned into the circle with linked arms. The last time her mother had taken her and her sister to see *The Nutcracker* she had been bored. From where they sat in the balcony, the dancers below looked like porcelain figurines. When they scissored their legs and leapt through the air, their lightness of spirit could not cut away her heaviness of heart. Instead, she had wondered at their powderiness, their pinned hair; at the self-forgetfulness it would take to allow one to be onstage, in timed motion, in character. It was hard enough to stay in character as yourself, she had thought then. Now she wondered if she knew who that self was. *What did _she_ want*, her therapist had asked last summer. From her window, she watched students scurrying in the cold below, snow catching on their coats, their bare heads, and knew they shared a secret that, lean in as she might, she could not fathom.

Twenty-Seven

There was no reason to invite the boy from Phil 8 to her room after seeing *La Strada* with him, except she couldn't get Gelsomina's face, the purity of her blind devotion, out of her head. She knew her, knew The Strongman, The Fool, intimately—by the shadows on their faces, the way they walked across the screen. Watching side-by-side with him had given her an illusion of closeness, as if, because their eyes were riveted on the same images and their elbows shared the same scratchy armrest, they must be seeing and feeling the same things. As if the movie linked them. *Every pebble has its purpose,* The Fool had told Gelsomina, sealing their fates. Nothing in art moved her more deeply than human vulnerability, even as, already pinned, she struggled to deny her own. Blind devotion, blind desire: the closeness had been inside her head until, regrettably, enacted, it evaporated, leaving her to pump him like a blood pressure bulb while he searched haphazardly for her body's magic code, its open sesame. What had happened to the inner conviction, the knowing, she had once felt and followed? Spontaneity guaranteed nothing. *I told you so*, said her better judgment, defiled, and even to her, the *What difference does it make* that she automatically shot back sounded hollow. Just like a man, she never wanted to see him again.

Twenty-Eight

She and the boy from Teaneck lay on their stomachs on his bunk bed, listening to music and reading, she near the wall, and he on the open side, so he could jump up and change a record before the next track started. Although he did without a typewriter and wrote all his papers by hand, he had a library of LPs arranged in alphabetized boxes lining the edge of the bed—a fraction of what he stored back home. They were studying together, she reading Hume, he the poets of the Harlem Renaissance, but she could hardly get through a page undistracted. The waterfall of a giggle melodically trilling through his laughter wasn't exactly girlish, and the toss of his hair as he provided background on each song and artist not quite diva-like, but the hint of girlishness, of incipient diva-hood, like the little gold stud in one ear, the amber he rubbed on his wrists, created in her a delirium. She couldn't decide if what moved her was masculinity softened by the feminine, or innate femininity overtaking the masculine—a shawl of Spanish moss blithely flung across a cypress, or the cypress merely a frame on which to display the tapestry of moss. She relished the indeterminacy, relished that he too had secrets. She liked thinking they were both different from the other students she knew. When finally he turned toward her, it was to place a mustache twirled from the ends of her hair under her nose. Kissing him was like being blindfolded and spoon-fed something delicious, not quite familiar, unplaceable: brandied pears or brandied apples? Hazelnut or mocha mousse? She could never name what made his languid kisses so sweet—before he broke them off to exchange Esther Phillips for Mabel Mercer.

Twenty-Nine

Reading Marx's *18th Brumaire* over lunch, she looked up to ponder a passage that gave her pause—"Men make their own history, but they do not make it just as they please"—and noticed two boys to her left talking in rising tones of glee and disbelief. They were recounting a story a friend had told them, a story about a girl who had, for no apparent reason, brought him to her room after the movies, seduced him, and then closed the door on him, as if he'd just delivered pizza. Mortified, she listened as they reeled between vilification and envy, chewing the story to bits. Who were they to judge, she muttered to herself, glowering. She was tempted to interrupt them, to say, *Excuse me, that was me, what of it?* Then she would tell them the story from her perspective, which was different, of course, and simple: she had squandered herself on him. Well, she wasn't going to martyr herself over a one-night stand. Shielding her eyes, her burning cheek, as if from the room's fluorescent glare, she put her head back down in the posture of reading, and kept listening until she was sure they hadn't been given any clues to her identity. Long after the boys were gone the words played themselves over and over in her head, like a language drill, embedded in her memory. She fucked him blind. *Bien trouvé.* He could have been a delivery boy. *Bien vu.* She fucked him blind. *Bien trouvé.* A real case. *Bien vu.* She fucked him blind. *Bien . . .* To escape the loop, she picked up her highlighter and began reading the xerox where she'd left off: "The tradition of all dead generations weighs like a nightmare on the brain of the living." *Bien entendu.*

Thirty

It was no coincidence, as she first thought, that, like a phantom from the past, her boyfriend from boarding school was standing outside her dorm, just as he used to before the morning assembly. How had he got there? She hadn't realized his college was only a few hours away by train. He had been serenading all night, he told her; had thrown pebbles up to her window but none had reached high enough: each hit the brick below and skittered down to his curses. He had stood vigil, waiting for her to enter the building or leave it; had scrutinized countless mufflers in search of her face, about to give up when finally she walked out, right into him, at the bottom of her steps. She was incredulous and swept up at the same time. It was like reading *The Star*; she ended up believing some fraction of it must be true. Why hadn't he called first? He gave her his silly sheepdog look, so that he resembled the collage she had made of him in high school, and half-mockingly took up her hands: what if she had said she wouldn't see him, what would he have done? *Don't be ludicrous,* she laughed, releasing her hands, knowing it was true; it would have been easy, easier anyway, to say no on the phone. But seeing him in person made her feel known, as if she'd been stranded, an émigré, and he alone, among all those swirling around her, could understand her. After a year and a half, she had forgotten how suffocated she used to feel, and was warming again to his *I'm-harmless* charm. By this time they were standing at the edge of the yard, under an archway, facing each other. *Just coffee,* he pleaded, though he didn't need to. *Just coffee,* she agreed.

Thirty-One

He came back the next weekend, bringing her a red rose bought
near the kiosk, already vased, a flask of Jamaican rum, and hot
chocolate mix. It eased her homesickness to reminisce about old
teachers and friends while sipping spiked cocoa on her single bed.
The Paul Klee poster above her desk, a man's rotund head in pinks
and oranges with his bow tie askew, looked across the room at them
enigmatically. She had been trying to write about it the week before
but something had eluded her. It wasn't enough, she realized now,
letting him refill her mug, to describe just the surface, which anyone
could see. You had to go beyond it and bring up the ineffable, the
unexpected, the truth that startled. Recognition, then surprise: the
comfort of the familiar, the lull of the known—then the dis-ease
of discovery, the bayonet of the strange. Did she crave them both
equally? She guessed she lurched between them. She was in her head,
contemplating the poster, sipping her chocolaty rum, when he began
whispering in her ear all the sweet things she had imagined no one
would ever say to her again. She shouldn't have been surprised, but
surprise, spiked with relief, was half the pleasure—the other half,
showing off without explanation how naturally it now came to her
to move her hips.

Thirty-Two

She had told her parents she wouldn't be coming home for Thanksgiving even before she had plans. She didn't want to be scrutinized: her eating habits and weight assessed, her feelings dismissed as moods. At first they had reluctantly accepted her reasoning that California was too far to go for a long weekend, but when on their next Sunday phone call she told them she would be going to New York to visit her old high-school boyfriend, they tried to convince her to change her mind. The trains would be delayed and crowded; the ice slippery. It was a family holiday—her sister was coming from an equal distance. She sighed. She knew it was her mother's favorite holiday. When they sensed her weakening they changed angles: to topple a tree you had to get at it from all sides. Why take up with him again? Hadn't they heard her being dismissive of him many times? But that was none of their business, a miscalculation. It toughened her resolve and she managed to get off the phone without making a commitment. The next day she called back, armed with information: it was too late to get a flight home; the dorms would be closed; she had to go somewhere; they could call his mother. Although she'd never met her, she imagined she was eager for him to have a steady girlfriend and would say all the right things.

Thirty-Three

Sitting cross-legged on the floor, she shuffled the girl's deck three times, as instructed, then cut it into three sections before putting it back together with the left-hand pile on the bottom, the right-hand pile in the middle, and the middle on top. Then she spread the cards out and hesitated. They were in the girl's dorm room, the bookcase and bed decorated with gypsy scarves and antique lace. She had to choose three cards. Not Past/Present/Future, but Situation/Self/Challenges. She delayed, forcing her hand to pass over cards that lay apart and caught her eye, instead ferreting out one that was visible only by a sliver, another by a corner, a third, a thin horizon. She didn't want to look at the cards once she turned them over; she felt strangely ambivalent, as if they were going to show her herself once and for all, and though she craved nothing more, the prospect terrified her. Instead, she watched the girl across from her brood over the images. Her eyes were an extraordinary blue, a bit watery, like vitreous marbles put under a faucet to bathe away the dust. At last she spoke, in a voice no different from her everyday one: husky, warm, matter-of-fact. *Consumed by fear and indifferent to it, you are in danger,* she said, *of complacency, stagnation. But past patterns that confused you can be gotten over.* The girl smiled. *Does that make sense?* Finally looking at the cards she had chosen, she was startled by the medieval figures wielding clubs that sprouted green leaves on one card, balancing discs engraved with five-pointed stars on another, and on the last, pierced halfway to the hilt by swords. The words made her twitch, and she searched for their justification in the imagery before her, but her heart was leaping like a trout trying to escape the lure it had already swallowed. She nodded. She knew the words had meaning. Whatever she took them to mean.

Thirty-Four

Especially when he wasn't there, it was a relief to have a boyfriend. It helped her relax; she could flirt or walk away after class as she chose, without every encounter being fraught with innuendo. Over Thanksgiving, she let him slip into the role—how else to respond to his family's acceptance of her in his attic room, their welcoming her to their table? Not that she was at ease when his father said grace and gave thanks for their happiness as a family, knowing as she did that he spent most nights at his office, sleeping on a pull-out couch with a former student, while the mother rarely let him through the double-bolted door. She tried not to gawk, but she had never before thought about adults, *parents*, having secrets and tempests; she marveled at their poise, and emulated it by yielding to their son, demurring with only the slightest off-key laugh as he presented her to the other guests as his fiancée.

Thirty-Five

She was helping his mother and sisters clean up, drying dishes and stacking them on the counter, when her father called to wish her a happy Thanksgiving. She could tell from his voice that her parents had been waiting for her to call. As they chatted his voice grew more barbed. *I'm sure you'd like to talk to your mother,* he said, *but her sinuses are bothering her and she's gone to lie down. We may end up having our turkey tomorrow.* No matter where she stood, as far as the phone cord stretched, there was a cabinet in front of her that his mother or a sister needed to open as they milled around, putting dishes away, pretending not to listen. *I hope you're enjoying your Thanksgiving,* he continued, *because you ruined ours.* Her father never trusted her to put two and two together; he liked to spell everything out. *I'm having a nice time,* she finally said, with an eye to the kitchen, *but of course I miss being home too. Please tell Mom I'm sorry she's not feeling well,* she added, flattening herself against the counter to let his sister by with the turkey platter.

Thirty-Six

He didn't want to bother going downstairs to the boys' bathroom, so to the inconvenience of the girls on her floor, they showered together. *Why don't you wash inside yourself—do you think you're a self-cleaning oven?* he asked abruptly one morning, watching her soap her thighs. Taken by surprise, she didn't know quite what to say, but his words hovered in her mind like kitchen flies over a bowl of ripe apricots: she could swat them away but every few moments they'd reland, distributing the spoilage. Badgering her was part of a larger campaign to get her back on the pill. He hated the way she groped for her diaphragm with one hand as soon as they began to kiss, stopping completely to spread the spermicide around the edges and slopping a big dollop, like crème fraîche, in the middle, before inserting it and resuming. As they hung up their towels, she tried to hide her fluster by laughing it off, but from then on began as a matter of course when he was visiting to put in her diaphragm in the toilet stall, after brushing her teeth.

Thirty-Seven

To celebrate having submitted poems for the spring semester's beginning poetry workshop, she invited the poet to a woman's bar. They were crossing the river on the T when she confessed, to the poet's amusement, that she had found it difficult to put the submission packet together. She had wanted to write about Spain, but kept seeing her mother's bent head, her helmeted coiffure, embedded in the fabric of the page, like a watermark. *How peculiar,* the poet mused, so she told her how her mother had read her journal but denied it for weeks. *Why not write about what your mother did,* the poet said as the doors opened with a hiss of steam and they stepped onto the concrete platform. She herself wrote swiftly, ruthlessly, and was proud of her lack of writer's angst. *You need to exorcise it. It's the keystone; once it falls, all your inhibitions will come tumbling down.* She thought it over. She could hardly imagine what it would be like to write about any of it. By then they were in an industrial neighborhood, walking under an overpass. The poet took her arm as they concentrated on finding the unmarked door.

Thirty-Eight

Walking in, the poet held on to her arm: like the cat about to eat the canary, she was trying not to appear overtly, prematurely, elated: The Nonesuch, at least among student rowers and radical feminists, was infamous. Though no one looked twice when they sat down at the bar and ordered two wine spritzers, she found herself surreptitiously staring. She wasn't surprised to see muscular women in hiking boots, plaid flannel shirts, and jeans, but she hadn't expected women in low heels and conservative dresses; women who set their hair. One of them, tall and lanky, in an open-necked silk chiffon blouse and cuffed crepe pants, transfixed her. The woman epitomized everything she herself was not: alabaster coolness; the mysterious pull of detachment. She wondered what it would be like to reveal herself, be intimate, with such a creature, a gazelle more unapproachable than any man. Would a creature that composed, naked, also be vulnerable, pliable, yearning? Now, on the small black-and-white-checked dance floor, it was the alabaster woman who stared at them swirling to the robotic beat, like dervishes disrupting a military parade. The music paused. The poet yawned. It was time to go. Up from the subway, back on their side of the river, cheery with vague excitement, the poet thanked her with a kiss so soft it imprinted her imagination more deeply than her lips.

Thirty-Nine

Koko Taylor was on the turntable, but they weren't studying: they were sitting cross-legged on his bed playing cat's cradle with a bootlace. He had wanted to hear every last detail about the lesbian bar and seemed disappointed that she hadn't gone home with, as he called her, Marlene Dietrich, or at least the poet. Sometimes, fleetingly, she wondered whether he encouraged her to fantasize about women so that she wouldn't fantasize about him. It protected them both, even as it bound them. She worried that if she exposed the depth of her desire he would refuse her. One night over dinner, when friends of her parents had been visiting, she'd overheard the man say to her father, nodding his head at her: *She looks like a wild one. I bet you have to hold the reins tight.* At the time, it made her furious, but since then she'd often turned it over in her mind. Herself a wild horse. The bit still in, but the reins flying. She wiggled her toes. She didn't feel wild. He was rubbing her foot, the bootlace dangling down his fingers. But she was hobbled, and kept herself from telling him how more than anything she wanted him to kiss her instep.

Forty

She woke to the sound of her boyfriend's voice, low and gruff, in her ear. They were staying in a motel: he had grown tired of stumbling, on his way to the john in the middle of the night, through the dark outer room where one of her roommates slept. Stirring, she felt his weight on top of her, and remembered noticing, as their cab crossed the bridge the night before, that the river was frozen. Daggers of ice hung from the motel's eaves; on the way to their room, she had slipped on the slick path. His voice, her name, grew sharper, more insistent. Catching her hand as she lifted it over her head, he broke her stretch, as the night before he had broken her fall. Grateful then, she found it irritating now. Her lids were stuck together, jammed. And something was jamming her knuckle; something was trying to jam its way inside her. Snatching back her hand, she jerked up against the headboard, toppling him. A tiny clatter trembled the nightstand. Finally she opened her eyes. *I wanted to surprise you,* he said, slumped over his erection on the shag rug, searching for the ring.

Forty-One

At first she wouldn't talk to him at all. But he kept pounding on the bathroom door, rattling the knob, shouting. Finally she said, *It's a thin door, you don't have to shout,* and they stayed like that, one on either side of it, for an hour. Shivering, she had wrapped herself in a towel, but as he talked she opened the towel and sat on the counter, looking at herself in the mirror. She had hardly seen herself in months: in the dorm everyone dried off in the shower; no one stood at the mirror naked to brush their teeth. *I want to marry you,* he repeated. She didn't see any bruises, and he hadn't come. *I want to marry you.* She took her diaphragm out and rinsed it in the sink, put it on a washcloth to dry. Her body might be unmarked, but she knew it wasn't a blank page: it had been written and written on, so densely, one phrase on top of the other, from birth on, that the words ran together. The scrape on her elbow: that came from a bicycle fall. The pressure in her chest? Was that his handwriting or her own? What about the way her nipples tingled in the cold air? She remembered someone trying to crack one like a walnut between his teeth, someone else licking them like foam. Perhaps, under the right conditions, in the right light, she could peel off one layer at a time to decipher. *At least keep the ring,* he said before he left, *at least don't forget me.*

Forty-Two

At the carousel, waiting for her bags, her mother first noticed the gold hoop earrings she had bought for herself, then the silk cord peeking out from under her collar. Without thinking she needed to ask, she touched the hoops lightly, and pulled the cord up like a line from a fishing hole, to see what had been caught between her daughter's breasts. She couldn't help laughing at the tiny gold band with two hands interlaced at the top—it looked like something adolescent girls might exchange—though seeing her daughter recoil she stopped herself from saying what she must have been thinking: such a tiny little fish, shouldn't you have tossed him back? *Hmm, what is it?* she said instead, her eyes narrowing. *Nothing, it's nothing, and it's none of your business,* she answered, giving her mother a dirty look as she yanked it back and tucked it inside her bra. After that, they both kept their eyes on the carousel as it went round and round, suitcases of all sizes clattering down.

Forty-Three

Her parents were ecstatic to have her home, but the lavishness of their praise burned like mockery; it made the girl who lurked beneath the college coed, the one everyone ignored as though she could be cold-shouldered out of existence, sullen. Sometimes, lost in her thoughts, she would run the ring from side to side, making the cord taut, or rub it against her lips, pushing her tongue through the center. She didn't know why she wore it, or what it was a talisman of. *It's like walking on eggshells being around you,* her mother complained after having her hand swatted away when she tried to fluff hair out of her daughter's face, and again, *eggshells,* each time she asked about the food, roommates, and classes, only to be curtly rebuffed. To tarnish their pride without calling attention to herself, she recited ad nauseam the sins of the institution that had so flattered them by accepting her—the labor disputes, land grabs, apartheid investments, huge lecture halls, poor student-teacher ratio; the inaccessibility, even senility, of its most renowned professors; the lack of tenured women—but they took it all in stride, marveled at her eloquence and laughed at her intensity, saying she had become a real college student: analytical, disaffected, holier-than-thou.

Forty-Four

She considered her mother's gifts a yardstick of her incomprehension of who her daughter was: lace nightgowns, eyelet blouses, and minty green sweater sets—things her mother fancied but that she would never wear. Finding a See's candy–sized box on her bed the day before she returned to school, she knew it couldn't be chocolates: at home her mother still monitored everything she put in her mouth. She rattled it. Solid and heavy. No doubt a book, a volume of inspirational verse to go with the one that lay untouched on her night table. Slipping the ribbon off, she looked at the card before carefully untaping the fleur-de-lys wrapping. *Dearest daughter,* it read, *all our love, Mom and Dad.* Sighing, she looked down to see what she held. Bound in leather, lined with marbled Italian paper, it was the most beautiful notebook she'd ever seen. She caressed its pages, cream-colored, smooth, *blank.* The irony enraged her. Did she think her trespass could be made whole so easily, forgiveness bought? Stomping through the house, she found her mother wiping crumbs off the kitchen counter with a dishcloth. *How dare you,* she said, waving the book like contraband in her mother's face. Her mother looked startled, as if woken from a reverie. *Keep it for yourself. I'd need a padlock, a trip wire, something foolproof to keep prying parents out. Or did you have it custom made with a homing device, so you'll always know what I'm thinking? Well, those days are over.* She placed the book on the damp counter. Disappointment crumpled her mother's face. *Dear,* she began, but her daughter cut her off. *It's perfect for your hearts-and-flowers world, but too deluxe for all the unspeakable things I'd put in it.* Besides, she added to herself, she didn't plan to ever keep a journal again.

Forty-Five

She stopped at the landing, looking for her friend from Teaneck, on the way up to her room. His door was open, and from the stairwell she could see bare ticking on the lower bunk and, underneath, where his albums had been, box marks outlined in dust. She put her bag down and walked in, but just as a vacated room doesn't reveal whether a patient has been wheeled out strapped to a stretcher or clutching his get-well cards and flowers, so his room, though it had not yet vanquished his absence, told her nothing of why he had vanished, or where he had gone. His disappearance frightened her, as if she too could, at any moment, evaporate without a word.

Forty-Six

In line to have her backpack inspected on her way out of the library, she felt a tap-tap on her shoulder. People's ways of tapping were like signatures or songs: those you know you recognize at once. This tap, jaunty and confident, asserted a familiarity that didn't yet exist. Annoyed at the presumption, she turned around, frowning, into the grin of the poet's old boyfriend, the *good* boyfriend who had been dumped. The epithet intrigued her. She remembered his playful swat when the poet poked him in the ribs. With her in common it was easy to imagine they were long-lost friends, and by the time they were carrying coffee mugs up to his room, the poet had slipped out of their conversation as deliberately and surreptitiously as a wedding band is dropped into a coat pocket. Lying underneath him, his breath like radio static in her ear, she counted his mechanical ins-and-outs like sit-ups, and silently encouraged him to reach his goal sooner rather than later. Nonplussed by her own detachment, she found herself questioning again what was so good about him. His loopy smile, perhaps, which had popped up now that he lay beside her. The way he was affectionately tracing the sweat between her breasts. How he presupposed that now they had an understanding. Shoulders hunched and hands jammed into her pockets, she found the poet's name in the rough edge of a ripped seam, and she said it over and over to herself as he kissed her good-bye, until finally she tore her mouth away and said it aloud. Should they tell her? *Makes no difference to me*, he said, *that's over.* Oh, that's good, she thought. *It will make a fun story. She's my friend.*

Forty-Seven

Her section leader had been calling every few weeks since she stopped going to his meetings, but usually one of her roommates answered and, recognizing his nasal whisper, said she was at the library. Surprised by his call early one morning, she feigned and stammered and equivocated, managing to get off the phone only by promising she would stop by his office with a list of what she didn't understand. Finals were just a week away. She had no intention of going, but thought that she probably *should* make a list and ask one of the science majors in the dorm to help her. Her problem with astronomy, aside from wanting to avoid her section leader, was that all the laws were so rich with meaning, she had trouble keeping her mind on the phenomena for which they were intended. She knew physics wasn't supposed to be applied to the world as experienced by people, but she found herself associating Einstein's theory of relativity with her repeated perception that no one ever agreed on what happened between them, and she couldn't read about black holes without stopping to brood about all that felt hidden and inaccessible inside her. *How can something disappear if it still exists?* she would ask herself. *Is it retrievable?* But the mind, she already knew, was like that, like a game of Snakes and Ladders. At any moment a thought could slip away, as if sliding down a garbage chute, to be lost to the landfill; and a memory, like one of the Hydra's heads, could spring up, two growing where one had been cut off. It chagrined her that she had been browbeaten into making a false promise, that she had no help for what she didn't understand.

Forty-Eight

The poet was licking mauve yogurt off her spoon when a mischievous smile flitted across her face. *I heard you ran into someone I know at the library,* she said, raising her eyebrows twice, like Groucho Marx. *Well, what do you think? Does he solve all your problems?* She scraped up more yogurt and smiled again, but this time her eyes were cold and challenging. He had told her, after all. What, she speculated, had he said? She should have known that no one wanted for a friend someone who ate her table scraps. Staring at her uneaten soup as if the floating bits offered a way out, she felt, weirdly, not like a betrayer, but like the betrayed, as though they had set her up, colluded against her, like a mark in a Henry James novel. Strengthened by this scenario, she rallied and picked up her spoon, dipping it down where the meat was. *I think once was enough,* she began, smiling with her full spoon in the air. *But,* and here she took her bite and looked up, to see how the poet would like being fed her own words, *you know, as you told me, I'm not beholden to anyone, not to you, not to him—only the truth.* The poet snorted. *The truth. Do you think you'd recognize it?*

Forty-Nine

He dropped out, he said, because he was pissed off. They were sitting at the bar of the restaurant where he worked. It had taken his old roommate days to find the scrap of paper with his phone number; she had called right away. He shook his head and poured them both more wine: *That bastard, all those bastards, they think they know so much.* He hadn't been formally accused of plagiarism, but his section leader thought his paper on the Harlem Renaissance "too good for a freshman, too good for block handwriting, too good to be true." She stared into her glass, as if hypnotized. Finally, she took a sip and looked at him: *But so close to finals, why not finish out the semester?* Sighing, he tipped the bottle back to study the label. *Too late. I've already informed the administration and I can't go back without reapplying. Anyway, waiting pays good money; I've got lots of time to myself, lots of time to read, to go to the museum, the discos, the Fens.* He grinned and looked up. *Spicy. Last year's zinfandel. Let's split another.*

Fifty

In the middle of the night, twisted up in the sheets of her own desire, she let the arch of her foot roll against his ankle as if by accident, but lay still as a mummy, listening to his light snore. It was excruciating, an exquisite torture, to lie next to him. For a moment she had thought they would make love, but now she knew it would never happen, not unless she took him in his sleep, or turned into a boy. It would never happen. She had been on her stomach, and he had slithered on top of her, kissing the back of her neck, rubbing her bottom through her unbuttoned jeans, but when she shrugged free of her blouse and pivoted over to return his kisses, he had tumbled off as if thrown from a horse. *Too much wine,* he had muttered, before turning away. So intense was her longing, even the most muted gesture she could think to make, like smoothing his hair back with one finger, seemed to her too insistent, and for an hour she lay with her arms crossed over her breasts, immobilized, her body its own straitjacket, her desire consuming, a fire flared by the water meant to douse it. Finally, ashes in her mouth, she climbed over him to get out of bed, letting her breasts flop and graze his back, his shoulder, his chest. *There,* she thought, *there and there.* Then she dressed and gathered her things. The copier was open all night. She could finish her xeroxing.

Fifty-One

At this hour, Gnomon's was empty. She couldn't see the sky from the plate-glass window, only the way the dormitories across the avenue loomed as they emerged, the cover of night thrown off. Once, in Spain, she had stayed on the beach all night with an Australian bartender and watched dawn stream over the mountains as he slept. She smiled to herself, idly perusing the message board, and was studying a basket of kittens captioned "We need a home" when the lank-haired Classics major walked in, her fingers stained blue, papers heaped helter-skelter in her arms. She often stayed up all night, the girl said, and they talked about how medieval the town felt at this hour, the cobbled streets free of traffic, the brick archways like sentry posts guarding the yard. Suddenly the girl began to cry. That boy, did she remember, they had talked about him? She dimly remembered. Well, she had taken her advice and slept with him. She had slept with him once, and since then he hadn't called. Her father was dying—she knew that too, didn't she?—but she had slept with the boy anyway, it was her first time, and now she felt awful, sometimes worse about the boy than about her father, and that in itself made her sick. She was pulling at the roots of her hair; papers were flying out of her arms. *You told me to do it,* she said finally. *You said, why not? Why agonize, why not see what it's like? Well, it's like this,* the girl said, jabbing her shoulder. *It hurt like hell and then off he trotted, leaving me worse than before. My father can't speak; the boy hasn't called; my mother won't let me come home.* "Not until after finals," *she says.* "Concentrate on your studies. He'll be just fine." *The girl jabbed her again.* He's not fine, he's dying. You think you know so much, but you don't know shit. Then, like an apparition, the girl was gone. *Is that how I seem?* she wondered, picking up the trail of papers the girl had left in her wake. When had she become so cavalier, so callous? She paid for her copies and walked to the Union for coffee. The sun was already up, weakly throbbing beneath the skin of clouds. It never rose shining here, but she knew from experience that later in the day, like a blister, it would break through.

Fifty-Two

The morning of her first exam, she woke early. She had, she decided, studied enough. If she didn't know it already, it was too late now. As she made her way to the Union, it began to snow, hushing her footfall, coating her nerves. There was time to walk down to the river and get breakfast on her way back up. She hardly ever walked there by herself; it frightened her a little. Men trolled the banks, some for other men, others for girls. She knew how easy it was to be drawn in, to end up somewhere she didn't expect, with someone she never meant to choose. But today, her wits about her, she walked with her hands stuffed in her pockets, snow tufting her hair, and let her feet lead her. Too many times what she thought she knew prevented her from seeing what was there. Was she most misguided when most certain or most uncertain? She would have liked to test that question against every facet of her life, but her exam was in two hours; she had to keep her head clear. As the snow intensified it began to swirl. She could see the river as through an overglaze. Reaching the grass, she stood still for a minute, trying to follow the trajectory of just one flake as it spiraled down. It was absurdly difficult. She knew that under a microscope each was unique, but here, on the riverbank, in the storm's flurry, she could no more tell one apart from another than the miller's daughter could have spun straw into gold. Roomfuls of straw into roomfuls of gold. Letting her arms blade through the air, she opened her mouth: as the flakes dissolved, sizzling on her tongue, the snow, the sloping bank, the river's iced surface, the steam cloud of her exhaled breath, all seemed to her a perfect, impermanent expression of the world.

BOOKS FROM ETRUSCAN PRESS

American Fugue | Alexis Stamatis
translated by Diane Thiel with Constantine Hadjilambrinos

Drift Ice | Jennifer Atkinson

Parallel Lives | Michael Lind

God Bless: A Political/Poetic Discourse | H. L. Hix

Chromatic | H. L. Hix (National Book Award finalist)

The Confessions of Doc Williams & Other Poems | William Heyen

Art into Life | Frederick R. Karl

Shadows of Houses | H. L. Hix

The White Horse: A Colombian Journey | Diane Thiel

Wild and Whirling Words: A Poetic Conversation | H. L. Hix

Shoah Train | William Heyen (National Book Award finalist)

Crow Man | Tom Bailey

As Easy As Living: Essay on Poetry | H. L. Hix

Cinder | Bruce Bond

Free Concert: New and Selected Poems | Milton Kessler

September 11, 2001: American Writers Respond | William Heyen

etruscan press

www.etruscanpress.org

Etruscan Press books may be ordered from:

Consortium Book Sales and Distribution
800-283-3572
www.cbsd.com

Small Press Distribution
800-869-7553
www.spdbooks.com